DANGEROUS LEGACY

"I still can't believe that our lives are in danger," I said.

"Your father may have told you that I have always been a sentimental man and one who is prone to see life in its most exaggerated proportions. While this has been a disadvantage, many times over the years it has proven to be almost second sight. Do you follow me, Daphne? You are so young. One gets feelings of danger, of apprehension that it would be foolhardy to ignore. I believe that two attacks on you have already been made." He looked at me questioningly.

I admitted it. "Yes, I suppose they were, grandfather. I simply was unable to believe it."

"Then we will each of us take precautions. At least until we can discover which of our relatives would want a larger share of the estate. You are in greater danger than I, I believe. After all, I am a very old man. My natural years are numbered. None of this surfaced until I sent for you. . . ."

Also by Esther Jane Neely:

SOUTH WIND
THE MOON CAT

CHATEAU LAURENS

ESTHER JANE NEELY

Book Margins, Inc.

A BMI Edition

Published by special arrangement with Dorchester Publishing Co., Inc.

If you purchased this book without a cover you should be aware that this book is stolen property. It was reported as "unsold and destroyed" to the publisher and neither the author nor the publisher has received any payment for this "stripped book."

Copyright © MCMLXXX by Esther Jane Neely

All rights reserved. No part of this book may be reproduced or transmitted in any form or by any electronic or mechanical means, including photocopying, recording or by any information storage and retrieval system, without the written permission of the Publisher, except where permitted by law.

Printed in the United States of America.

CHAPTER 1

A surprising ray of late sunlight shimmered upon the red tile roofs and chimney pots that made up the view from the bedroom of my suite at the Hotel France et Choiseul on the Rue St. Honoré in Paris. A bee, searching the geranium pots on the balcony, buzzed my ear with a simplicity of sound that started my tears again, just when I had regained composure and the courage to continue my sad journey to Strasbourg.

I had to go on. Wiping my eyes, I picked up and folded the long black cape and carried it into the sitting room to my open suitcase. At the sight of my name, Daphne Laurens, printed in father's precise and artistic hand, I shivered in a sudden paroxysm of fear for some inexplicable reason. Fear was one emotion I had not experienced throughout this journey. Grief and loneliness had overwhelmed the excitement of seeing Paris. The excitement that I would have known had father been traveling with me as we had planned before his death.

Premonitions and feelings of doom generally descended upon me on grey days, such as we had been having, as I toured gardens and monuments, art galleries and cathedrals; but on this evening, my next to last in Paris, the wind had changed. I felt that I was seeing the city for the first time. During most of my stay, it was covered with floating mists. The past two days the city had been particularly obscured by smoke from factory chimneys carried on northeasterly winds. Now the winds from the south-southwest, the prevailing winds, had returned, the fringed green-black limbs of the linden trees in the patio reached out to the lowering sun.

I stood looking at them, wondering about my sudden premonition. Perhaps my subconscious worried about the ordeal ahead—meeting so many relatives I had never known existed until my father's illness. Being an only child, raised by my grieving middle-aged father, Armand Laurens, I had been an introspective child. Father often said that I probably was psychic as my mother had been. In my teens he began to worry about my future and made efforts to bring out my natural brighter disposition.

At this time in his life, he had finally been accepted as an artist. His increasing commissions for paintings required extensive travel across the United States. Previously, he had left me at home in Taos, New Mexico under the care of any one of many Indian women from the nearby pueblo . . .

At the sudden striking of bells nearby, I glanced at my watch. It was four-thirty. The American Express mail window closed at five. I snatched up my purse and umbrella, which I'd carried every day since I had arrived. Back home, grey skies forecast rain. Leaving my assorted clothing still unpacked and my suitcases open, I locked my door and ran down the lovely stairway to the delightful patio where delicate metal tables were arranged under colorful umbrellas and where trees and flowers grew in pots of all sizes. In the dining room overlooking the patio, waiters in white coats laid the fine white linen cloths for dinner.

I turned left into the arcade to leave my key with its heavy ornamental handle with the concierge.

"One moment, Mademoiselle Laurens. The post has come."

He pulled from my key-slot, a long orchid envelope which I instantly recognized. My grandfather, Claude Laurens, had written to me in America from Strasbourg, where I would soon go, advising me of places to visit in Paris. And always, which grieved me, he told me of his deep regret that my father had died before he could make this planned trip. This saddened me further because it was not until my father's illness was diagnosed as terminal, that I took it upon myself to write to my grandfather to tell him that his youngest son had regretted their bitter parting during World War II, and wanted to come home for a last visit.

An exuberant letter had come in one of the orchid envelopes, bearing the family crest, that delighted father. He said his father's pride of lineage had continued in times of his worst adversities. I gathered from this that father had somehow kept track of his family although he had never told me anything about them until we started planning our trip.

When father died I had to cable the sad news to my grandfather. An answering cable urged me to carry out my father's plans, and to my horror, begged me to accompany his remains for burial in the family plot at Chateau Laurens, outside of Strasbourg. A grieving letter in one of the orchid evelopes had followed begging me to comply. To do so, I was to travel as father and I had planned by freighter to the port of Rotterdam and transfer to a Rhine River cruise ship to Strasbourg.

Back there, alone in our small Taos home filled with the delicate paintings of my father's, I knew that I could not bear to travel all that long distance by sea with my

7

father's casket resting in one of the ship's holds. Our travel agent made the arrangements. Father's wish would be fulfilled. He would travel to Rotterdam by ship. I was advised by our family physician, and the travel agent, as well as friends to fly to Paris and do some of the things my father had wanted me to do.

In grieving shock, I followed the hearse to the small Santa Fe depot of Lamy where he was put aboard the train for New York and the freighter.

In a daze, I returned home to repack for my flight to Paris. I had decided to cancel all the side trips father had planned and to remain in Paris until time to meet the Rhine boat.

After a lifetime of knowing nothing about my father's family, I had only recently understood his grief, which I had always assumed was caused by mother's death at my birth. In his last days, I recognized his deep love for his native land and for his family. There is a closeness of French families unlike any other in the world. A Frenchman would go to any length to keep every member under his own roof. Father had done the unforgivable. He had married the beautiful Elsa Weill from Freiburg, a town across the river in the Black Forest of Germany whom he had met at the Sorbonne where both studied art.

Unhappily for the young couple, father's family had refused to accept Elsa. That was at the beginning of World War II. Father refused to fight against his wife's people. Torn and heartbroken, they fled to the United States. In the second year of that country's entry into the war, father had joined and gone across to do his small part to help France. And sorrowfully, he returned to his adopted country, to the far reaches of their hiding place high in the Sangre de Cristo Mountains, to find mother ill with tuberculosis. With the proper medication and care, she regained health slowly and lived until my birth when she was thirty-five.

And now, here I was, in France, soon to travel to my father's home to meet relatives of both my father and mother.

I placed the orchid envelope in the side slip of my purse. I hurried out through the arcade to Rue St. Honoré to the crowded Rue de la Paix, where I turned left to hurry up that fabulous street to Boulevard des Capucines. That well-known crossroads had become my favorite in Paris. Every day after picking up mail from Taos, I would return here from the American Express office in Place de l'Opera, sit at one of the many streetside tables of the Cafe de la Paix to read the letters; to gaze with awe and wonder at the hundreds of people, cars, taxis, buses; and to love the colorful kiosks and flower stands.

Although father had chosen Hotel France at Choiseul for old memories, we had planned many trips including the Loire Valley chateaux tour he and mother had taken as students, all of which I had cancelled. Our previous arrangements were to have all mail go to the American Express and not to hold our suite at the hotel while we were on our tours.

At American Express, I ran down the mobbed stairway, squeezing past students coming and going in the usual disorder and laughter, the joyous or the sad faces, depending upon their mail from home. I believe we all came late in order to be sure all of the day's mail had been put up.

When I finally got to the window, I spoke my name clearly, Daphne Laurens. Since it was almost time for the window to close, I decided to come back the next morning to fill out a forwarding slip and pay the small amount required for forwarding mail. As I turned with my small packet of letters, a tall young man near the wall smiled and made his way toward me through a surge of young people. I have always suffered from claustrophobia. More than once as a child I had panicked in crowds and father would swing me to his shoulders.

I had to get out. As I tried to make my way, the umbrella hanging from my arm bumped a hand. I felt a sharp pain in my arm and gasped as blood flowed from my ripped jacket sleeve. A young man, probably a fellow American, was now at my side. He looked at my sleeve, held me and glanced around wildly at the departing crowd.

Still holding my arm, he asked, "What happened?"

"I don't know. Perhaps someone held a letter opener . . ."

Pushing up my sleeve, he dabbed at the wound with his handkerchief. "Look here, that's a knife wound. There's a nurse on duty here. Let her look at it."

As he led me down the corridor to the nurse, he leaned toward the stairway and looked over the young people again.

"My accident made you miss getting your mail. The window's closed now. I'm sorry."

"It doesn't matter. The point is that that is a stab wound from a very sharp knife."

The young man leaned down to examine the wound as the nurse cleaned it. "I'm a medical student at Heidelberg. I think it was deliberate. If you hadn't made that quick turn, that knife would have gone into your back and probably to your heart. Would someone want to kill you?" He spoke rather precise English. The nurse looked up, startled.

I smiled at her as I answered. "Certainly not. I don't know anyone in Paris. I'm sure it was an accident. I moved too quickly."

Looking relieved, the nurse deftly bandaged my arm.

The young man lighted a cigarette and handed it to me. From deep in my shocked memory came a pair of burning eyes, eyes that had seemed to glitter pure hatred at me through very strong thick-lensed glasses. I remembered thinking that the young man must be frantic for a letter from home or from his girl. I couldn't bring back any other feature, only the eyes and glasses. I had found in the eyes what father used to refer to as natural cruelty.

"You've thought of someone," my new friend said, shaking his rather old-looking wise head.

"Probably imagination, but one young man in that crowd looked at me as if he were furious."

The nurse laughed as I got up. "He could have been if you stabbed him with that lethal-looking umbrella tip."

We all looked down and laughed. The metal tip of my umbrella was sharp and could have given someone a painful jab.

As we walked back toward the mail room I noticed that my new friend scanned the faces of every man we passed.

He took my arm. "You need a brandy. There's a café across the street."

"Café de la Paix? I go there every day to read my mail."

Although I loved going there alone, today I was glad to have Michael Strange from Boston with me. He led me adroitly across the street. Usually, I ran in terror.

After my calm life on our almost somnolent street of dust, traffic frightened me. I had traveled in my late teen years with father to many cities, but nowhere had the traffic seemed so wild.

We had now properly introduced ourselves, and finished our brandy when Michael said, "I still don't like this. I have always felt that young girls shouldn't come to Paris alone, or to any strange country. However, you seem to have survived. Your eyes are clear now. You looked dazed over there. I think we should have dinner together. If someone is out to kill you, at least you'll have a bodyguard for the evening. I leave for Heidelberg tomorrow."

He had been doing some work at the Sorbonne and was returning for summer classes. I had already decided that he was a determined and dedicated student who would make a fine doctor.

"Have you been ill?"

"No, I . . ."

He got up. "You look like a person in shock, and you didn't lose that much blood. You act like a person who hardly knows what she is doing."

I sat looking up at him. He had described me perfectly. Ever since my father's illness was determined terminal, I had been lost in a daze of being alone in the world, in grief at losing the only person in the world that I deeply loved, and worse yet, the only one who loved me.

I thought of our many friends in Taos who had led me through those last terrible days, had helped me finish packing . . . as we slowly walked down the tree-lined Rue de la Paix. By now, he was talking to me about my health and sounding much like father in the old days.

The concierge was concerned about my condition and for the first time I realized that I had walked all that distance with my blood-stained jacket sleeve. He inquired if I needed to go to the hospital. I reassured him as Michael sat down to wait for me at one of the lovely tables in the patio.

I was grateful for a friend, especially for one who spoke English. I could understand French but did not speak it well. Father had become almost totally American in his ways except, as he used to say, "Wine at meals," and rarely encouraged me with French.

I gave my suit to the dear little old lady in black, Yvonne. She had been lovely to me since my arrival, taking special interest in the fact that I preferred to retain the entire suite for my stay rather than move into a smaller room. These rooms were small, but I liked having the parlor where I kept my luggage, and where at night I had got into the habit of eating a light meal of white wine and the wonderful French bread and cheese while watching the doves settle in their nests in the eaves of the faded orange-red roof tiles.

It was still early evening as I strolled with Michael through the Place de la Concorde. He had departed from his serious mood and entered into a delightful if somewhat bloody account of the guillotine deaths of Louis XVI and Marie Antoinette. I stopped him as he started on Lavoisier.

"All right, then I shall tell you about the obelisk. It weighs 230 tons, is believed to be 3000 years old, was given to France by the Viceroy of Egypt, traveled here unbroken by ship, an amazing feat in that day and time with little equipment to move monstrous articles."

I looked up at the obelisk, and then at him. I had not noticed how handsome he was until now with the sun striking his very blonde hair and eyebrows. His blue eyes laughed down at me, and he gave my hand a squeeze.

"So now you understand that if I run out of money and can't become a world renowned surgeon, I can be a tour guide in Paris."

We strolled in the lovely birdsong world of the Gardens of the Tuileries, past fountains and statues of gods and horses. We sat down on a bench facing the Seine. The pavements were moist, exuding the last of winter's damp. Spring's candles, unshrouded, bloomed exalted on chestnut limbs. Buildings were expanses of sun-washed light. The lowering sun spread a rose glow which turned the smoky stone to pink, the slate rooftops to purple, black chimneys to orchid. Orchid. My mind, slow-witted by grief, remembered grandfather's letter. I looked in the slot in my purse. The letter was gone. I opened the purse and searched.

"Lose something?" Michael asked.

"A letter came to the hotel from my grandfather in Strasbourg. I'm going there."

"When?"

"Tomorrow."

"Good, then let's hope we are taking the same train. Mine is the express . . ."

"I'm sorry. I'm not going overland. I'm taking the Ile de France to Rotterdam to . . ." I faltered as tears stung my eyes.

Michael frowned. "You'd better tell me everything. It will be good for you and it will clarify to me why you act as if you are drugged."

I sat twisting my hands until he took them in his strong cool ones and held them firmly. I told him about my father dying and the exchange of mail between me and grandfather. My last sentence almost frightened me to death; it came up out of my subconscious. "And I'm terrified."

"Terrified of your grandfather?" Incredulously.

"I don't know. I didn't even know I was going to say that. It just came out."

He shook his head. "It's no wonder. You've been walking around a strange city alone all this time thinking of that freighter crossing the ocean, and of the ordeal that lies ahead. You shouldn't have come alone."

His serious eyes showed concern over a stranger's problems. I knew then that he would make a fine doctor. I think I loved Michael in that moment. Perhaps as one would love a brother. I had known no other love than that which I had for father. It was bewildering. I had known Michael so briefly.

"I'm going with you tomorrow."

I looked up, startled.

He smiled. "There's no hurry for me to get back to Heidelberg. I enjoy the river trip, I'll see if I can get a reservation aboard. Write down the name of your ship." He tugged a pad and pencil from his pocket.

I hesitated, wondering at his offer, then wrote it.

"I can take a train from Speyer or Mannheim, whichever side of the river the ship stops."

"I think it stops at Heidelberg. Father spoke of our stopping there."

"It's on the Neckar. Some riverboats do go on up, but most of the larger ships stop at Speyer. The passengers go to Heidelberg by bus and catch the ship at Mannheim or Koblenz, depending upon the ship's itinerary."

Still I hesitated. "It's kind of you, Michael." I was confused. It would be good to have his company, but it would be expensive for him. It was too much to ask of a stranger.

We watched a Bateau Mouche pass, filled with tourists. He reached for his cigarettes. Inadvertently, I glanced down.

"I'm sorry. Your jacket pocket." There was a spot of blood on the bottom of it. As I reached out to show it to him, he moved. My hand touched the cloth.

"I have a spot remover that will take it out. Don't worry about it. You've turned pale again. You must get hold of yourself. You have an ordeal to face. Come on. I know you've wandered around the Left Bank. Let me give you my own special tour."

He was studying to be a doctor. He should have seen my terror. My hand had touched a knife, possibly the very knife that had cut so deeply into my arm.

We started to walk down the quay. The sun caught the rose window at Notre Dame. For the first time in my many walks I saw the true beauty of it. We hurried, almost running.

"This is the perfect time to view it from inside." He pulled me along. I told myself that a medical student might very well carry a knife. And, he had mentioned that he had been doing "some unsightly dissecting" that afternoon.

Something inside me told me that I should release my arm from his and run as fast as I could to the safety of my suite at the Choiseul. We were passing the Prefecture De Police, on the Ile de la Cité. I looked up at Michael's face. Of course he had a knife for dissecting. He had no reason to want to kill me. I was being silly...

CHAPTER 2

It spite of my cringing horror at Michael's tales of the guillotines and the revolutions, his vast knowledge of the history brought to life the Ile de la Cité and Ile St. Louis, those beautiful islands that separated the Seine, far more than my guide book or various tours had been able to do. From the top of the Eiffel Tower they had looked like two floating ships. I had also viewed them from my Bateau Mouche tour of the Seine.

A few stalwart fishermen still lingered along the quays. Many couples were strolling now. I gloried in the lights of Paris that were now coming on. I had not ventured out after dark. The concierge had warned me not to. He had suggested that I take a night tour and see either the Lido or the Follies Bergere, but my heart wasn't up to gaiety. I had obeyed the concierge. Whatever else I am, I am not courageous.

Michael continued his tour-guide lessons as we strolled among the beautiful homes on Ile St. Louis, so like a town in itself. "This is more recent history. Something all girls are interested to know." He stopped and pointed, "This is where Helena Rubenstein lived."

We were laughing. My fears had subsided. I knew that no one in all of Paris knew of my existence and certainly no one had any reason for wanting it to cease. I had merely whirled too quickly from the mail desk and struck scissors or some sharp instrument someone held. As for robbing me, my purse could easily have been snatched. It had not been . . . My grandfather's letter . . . Impressive looking as his orchid envelopes are, I'm sure no one took it. I lost it.

As we walked along the quay on the Left Bank, Michael introduced me to a number of book stall operators who were his friends.

At a broad boulevard intersection he stopped in his guide's guise. "Now, in the most recent revolution, spring 1969, I was standing right here when the tear gas was flung into my group, which was not taking part, incidently. It was raining. I did not know until late that night that my feet and the feet and legs of most of my friends had been badly burned."

"Burned?"

"Yes. From the combination of tear gar and water. We were hospitalized. I wore bandages for weeks."

The café Michael had chosen for dinner was near the School of Medicine of the Sorbonne on the Boulevard Saint Germain. He led me inside. The wind had picked up and was almost cold. The tables had shining white cloths instead of the gaily colored ones outside, now whipped by wind and being collected by scurrying waiters. The silver and glasses were sparkling clean. The fragrances from the kitchen made me almost faint as I remembered that I had had nothing since my little lady in black brought croissants and the delicious French hot chocolate that morning.

Michael ordered Campari, hearty onion soup and an Alsace Riesling wine. The soup was the most delicious I have ever tasted. I was delighted when it was served in a heavy pottery bowl. This was exactly the way father taught me to serve it at home, after he taught me how to make it. Mine was never this good. This was thick with brown slivers of onion, thin broth and heavy with delicious cheese. French bread is always heavenly.

When the wine was placed in the metal ring beside the table, Michael lifted it and held the label turned for me to read. He had graciously ordered my grandfather's wine, Alsace Reisling of the Chateau Laurens Vineyards.

"I had no idea," I stammered.

"I didn't think you did. It's a favorite in France. This particular vintage is not his best, however. I connected it immediately when you described the envelope you lost with this crest." He pointed to it on the label.

All around us students and French families were dining on similar light menus. Father had always insisted upon our main or heavy meal being served at noon.

"What do you do back in Taos, New Mexico, Daphne?"

"I run a small shop. A friend has taken over while I am away." I told him that I started the shop before my father's paintings had become successful. I was thirteen. Many of my friends were girls from the pueblo who made beaded bags and headbands and bracelets. They tried to teach me but I had never been good with me hands. I had always known most of the Indian men and women who sat along the building fronts selling their wares. That was how I started. He leaned his head back and laughed.

"You've got the right coloring. Don't tell me you wore Indian costumes and pretended you were one."

"Of course not. But it did something for me. I had always been terribly shy. I found through this work that I loved to be with people, to meet strangers. Eventually I rented a shop. I sell paintings for the local artists."

He had never been to Taos and soon had me describing the area, especially the Sangre de Cristo range.

Then came a lovely surprise. A minute glass of Framboise, a delectable liqueur distilled from raspberries, a luxury my father had indulged in for as long as I could remember. I clasped my hands in delight.

Michael reached across the table to touch my hand.

"When you are animated in this way . . ."

"The wine. I'm not used to so much. We have it at home, but just one glass at dinner and with our evening meal."

He smiled. "I'm not sure now that it is the wine. I suspect this is the real you when you are not grieving. When you are like this you remind me of my sister. She is small like you, with an oval face, but not tanned as you are . . ."

"I've faded. All this dreary weather."

"Her eyes are dark too, but not as large as yours, nor are her lashes and brows as thick. And she also has dark hair."

My hands flew to my hair which I wore short and capped to my face. The damp weather of Paris had done nothing for it and I was certain I could stand some repairs. "I'll bet her hair isn't this awful."

"No. She has long hair which she used to wear in pigtails, and now in a chignon."

"I'd like that. She must be very nice."

"More so lately. In childhood she was impossible, ill natured . . . But I know that her physical disfigurement has been my reason for studying medicine. I want to be a surgeon, I want to perfect an operation to improve her back."

His eyes were so pained that I didn't ask him anything further about his sister. The fact that I reminded him of her assured me that he had come to my rescue at American Express for that reason.

By the time we had reached the street he had begun his light-hearted lectures.

"A question always asked by my clients is 'Why is this called the Latin Quarter?' To ward off that question I shall explain. In early years of the Sorbonne students and professors had to speak Latin at all times."

"Gracious. And I haven't learned to speak French well."

"You will if you are going to be with your grandfather."

"He writes to me in English. I wonder where I lost his letter . . ."

"You said that it was addressed to your hotel. Someone will find it and post it again. The French are an exceptionally honest people. You'll probably find it in your mail slot."

"I hope it doesn't take too long or I'll be gone."

"I am going to try to get reservations to travel with you."

"It would be expensive for you."

"I'll enjoy the trip. I feel you shouldn't be alone, not after what happened at the American Express office."

"That was an accident. No one would want to harm me. No one has any reason to."

"There are lots of strange people in the world, and a good many of them in Europe as well."

At that moment we were surrounded by a group of students. Michael turned to me, and introduced me. "They are going to La Boite Noire, a discoteque, and want us to join them. This one has a small orchestra, not just a machine."

"I shouldn't. I should go back to the hotel."

He took my arm. "You'll enjoy it. The music is lovely."

We did go. The small cellar was jammed with students, much too dark for my comfort. Worst of all, Michael had to translate everything anyone said to me since I couldn't understand German.

"Why do they call you Fritz?"

"We are all students from Heidelberg. It is what you would call a nickname."

"You've been a student for a long time if you were here for the 1969 revolution."

"Yes, my schooling has been sporadic, interrupted by the necessity to work."

All through the evening it had been occurring to me that Michael was not an American, yet I couldn't think of any reason for his telling me that he was.

"Do you work back home in Boston?"

"Would you believe it if I told you that I am really a tour guide? I have always had excellent tutoring for languages, and I suppose a natural ability."

"How wonderful. And you must have studied history, too."

He swept me into a lively dance that I enjoyed. These friends of his were not dancing in the popular way that kept couples separated, and which made me feel like an exhibitionist. Suddenly it was good to hear laughter, and look upon youthful smiling faces. He had been right; it was what I needed . . .

It was after two when we returned to the street. I had never been out late in a city. There is a certain magic in lighted but almost empty streets. When a lone taxi swept past it was but a brief reminder of the day's heavy traffic. Here and there on benches, couples sat embracing. Street sweepers with large white cans sang at their work.

Posters whistled in the wind on closed news kiosks. Paris was so quiet I could hear our footsteps.

As we reached the quay, a brilliantly lighted Bateau Mouche swept past under our bridge leaving a lingering sound of laughter and a strain of music.

The air had turned quite cold and damp, making it even colder for someone used to a dry country. When I shivered in my light-weight black wool suit, Michael placed his arm around my shoulders. We walked close together through the wind-rustled trees of the Tuilleries.

At the arcade entrance to the Choiseul, Michael said again that he would try to get a reservation on the Rhine boat.

I did not know the strange old man on duty when I asked for my key. "When is the next mail delivery, please?"

"At nine in the morning. Good night, Mademoiselle." I detected his disapproval of my late hour which gave me a feeling of security. But it also made me miss father whom I knew had always been overly protective of me, which left me unprepared for life alone.

Yvonne had mended the sleeve, cleaned and pressed my grey suit and hung it on my light fixture. And she had left a pot of chocolate under a napkin.

The night air had cleared my head of my unaccustomed amount of wine. I made three trips through my suite looking for the lost orchid envelope although I felt that I was unduly upset over losing it. I sat for more than an hour reading the mail, mostly letters of sympathy from out-of-town friends and some who had been away from Taos when father died.

When I finally went to bed I knew that when I got home to Taos I would miss the soft down pillows, and the delightful custom of placing a delicately cut linen towel under my bedroom slippers at the side of the bed.

Except for the wind, Paris seemed silent. I knew there still must be that city throb, that buses still ran, taxis darted, and that beneath Paris the great trains of the Metro churned through their tunnels. Here in my room, there was no sound. Outside a dove crooned in the eaves. I was utterly sleepless. After a time that seemed hours, I heard far away clocks strike and bells ringing . . .

The rain began quietly, falling so softly that I thought it was wind in the patio trees. I lay dreading what lay ahead until the soft rain on the tiles became snow falling on our tile roof at home and I was chimerically transported into a dream where father and I were safely asleep there . . .

CHAPTER 3

I woke up at ten o'clock to the dismal sound of steady rain. My tray, placed long ago on the small table beside the door, waited for me. The chocolate was cold, but it was so delicious, I didn't care. This day would hang heavy because The Ile de France, a trans-European express to Rotterdam, did not leave until 6:43 that evening.

Apprehensively, I unpacked boots and my tan London Fog coat, and finished packing my suitcases.

I was anxious for the mail, hoping the orchid envelope had been found and remailed to the hotel. I stood staring out at the rain-drenched patio. I had to go to American Express to forward mail, and to inquire if my refund for the trips I had cancelled would be paid here or sent home to Taos.

Crossing the patio in rain was not as delightful as crossing it other days. An inch of water had already collected on the tiles.

I looked up at the empty slot when I handed my key to the concierge. "Has the mail been delivered?"

"Quite early, and it has been placed."

"I shall be leaving this evening. I lost that letter that came yesterday from my grandfather. I'll leave a forwarding address. If you would be so kind as to watch for it . . ."

"Certainly." He handed me a form to fill out and a folded note.

It was from Michael. "Due to bad weather there were cancellations. Meet me at Gare du Nord at 5:30. Try to be on time. I'll wait for your cab at the main entrance."

The frown on the concierge's face assured me that he had read the note and did not approve. I had told him that I didn't know anyone in Paris. It was then that he warned me about walking about alone and not venturing out after dark unless with a guided tour group.

I smiled at him. "It's quite all right. He is a medical student from home." That information brought on further disapproval. Stuffing the note in my purse, I headed once more for the American Express office. I sloshed along holding my umbrella low. The rain had greatly diminished the number of people on the streets, and hopefully, at the mail window.

There were only two boys on the steps, but groups were gathered along the wall of the first floor reading letters.

There was a line at the mail window. Looking at the pleasant faces it seemed impossible to me that anyone had tried to kill me yesterday so I decided to put it out of my mind.

This time I attended to my business, and went back downstairs to cash a number of traveler's checks. I had decided to offer to pay Michael's fare. I was far from rich, and had a payment soon due on our home in Taos, but Michael was struggling to pay his way through school and I was sure he could not afford to pay a large sum just to befriend another American in distress. His words about the weather on the Rhine made me realize that the trip would not only be a sad one but a gloomy one. Also, I would need money.

I went inside the Café de la Paix, ordered one of those wonderful ham and cheese sandwiches on French bread, and looked at my watch. It was still only one o'clock. The Louvre would be perfect for a rainy day. Although I had been there numerous times, I had not begun to see all the works of art. I had been particularly anxious to view Monet's Water Lilies. My father's work had the same delicate quality, we had been told. Each time I had attempted to visit the Orangerie where the exposition was viewed there had been great lines of tour groups.

But I was not to get there. As I crossed the wide expanse of Place de la Concorde, holding my umbrella against the wind, a car swept so close that I stopped. A man walking behind me bumped into me. As I turned to apologize, I stared straight through the thick lenses of his glasses into the frightening eyes of the man I had seen yesterday at American Express. I knew it was the same man although many swarthy types look alike. The same feeling of terror overcame me as a taxi stopped. Grabbing the door handle, I jumped inside.

I was so frightened that my teeth chattered as I said, "The Louvre, please."

"Doesn't open until two."

It was now one-thirty. I did not want to wait. I didn't want to mingle in strange crowds. I had the driver return me to the Choiseul.

To my relief, five o'clock came. I stepped into a taxi to go to Gare du Nord. I knew from my guide book that it was not a long ride, but at this hour and in heavy rain, traffic would be slow. And it was with greater relief that

I saw Michael's worried face and his soaked hair which had formed ringlets dripping into the upturned collar of his black raincoat. How big and sturdy he looked.

He took my bags from the driver as I paid my fare. He carried only a small black case which he tucked under his arm. As he lifted my large case, he groaned.

"What are you carrying to Strasbourg, rocks?"

"Three of father's paintings. He chose and crated them as a gift for my grandfather. I didn't want to ship them." The gilt frames were molded with intricate designs and were fragile. I wanted grandfather to have them perfect.

Although we had plenty of time, he hurried me along. He seemed distracted and kept looking around the crowds, as if he watched for someone. He told me to walk ahead of him and kept advising me the direction to take.

Once we were in line, he examined my ticket and got his reserved seat in the same coach. He had already decided that we would have dinner on board. It was so like traveling with father who had made all decisions and issued orders, that I was content.

I adored the train the instant we entered the luxurious coach. I had never been on a European train and was amazed that the aisle was on the side. Our compartment, which we were to share with four other passengers, all soaking wet, was glassed in with a sliding glass door. The seats were long, covered with blue plush, and had arm rests that could be lowered to separate the seats. Two luggage racks above were too narrow for my large case. Michael took it outside and down the corridor to a luggage compartment. Passengers entered and thrust open the window to permit porters to hand in their luggage.

Dinner was served in a pleasant car much like our dining cars at home. However, here the dining steward passed out cards with numbers and a time for us to appear, a more satisfactory way than standing in line. We were of the first group. While dining, Michael asked me about my arm.

"I'm sure it is all right. It hurts a little."

"I'll take a look at it when we board ship."

"Do you remember asking if I had noticed anyone at American Express? This afternoon I was on my way to the Louvre. I stopped suddenly. A man bumped into me. He had been walking directly behind me."

He leaned forward. "And you had seen him at American Express yesterday?"

"I had noticed his eyes which I would call wicked eyes."

Michael was intense. "Go on, what did he look like?"

"Michael, there are certain nondescript persons that you could look at a dozen times and not remember any of their features. All I noticed of his man after seeing him twice was that he was a swarthy type with cruel eyes. I can't even tell you their color." I was sorry now that I had mentioned the man except that in telling I had convinced myself that I imagined it. I had seen two different men. I was on edge.

Michael seemed ready to forget the man too, and began telling me about the country we were now passing through although except for occasional passing lights, I could see nothing through the heavy rainfall.

But when we returned to our car, he excused himself. He was gone for a long time. Once I glanced up as a shadow passed the glass door and saw him going in the other direction. Something furtive in his actions made me think he did not want me to see him. I knew then that he was looking at the other passengers on the train.

The second sitting in the dining car took the other passengers from our compartment. Closing my eyes, I listened to the singing of the wheels on the rails, to the desolate lashing rain on the windows. I knew that I must get a tighter grip on myself. I couldn't believe that father was gone. But I would have to face it when I boarded the ship.

Feeling tears welling up in my eyes, I removed grandfather's letters from my purse. In one that was given to me upon my arrival at the Choiseul he told me about my relatives who lived with him. I didn't know what to expect of any of them, but from his letters I knew grandfather was a kind and sensitive man.

I found the right letter. "Daphne, I am trying to accept the loss of my last son. Over these years I have prayed for word that he was alive and well. I would often wonder if he and Elsa had given me grandchildren. It will be good for me when you tell me that his life was happy. Here you will find life rather different from your life in New Mexico. How very far away that seems. And what a long sad journey you must be having. I should have urged you to fly straight to me.

"Living here you will find your Aunt Celeste, my son Alfred's widow. After Alfred was killed, Celeste moved here to become my housekeeper, and a fine job she has done. She has one son, your cousin-by-marriage, Pierre Lilliard, whose father was killed in a hunting accident when Pierre was less than a year old. He is like a son to me.

"Your father would be saddened to know that his brother Jean died of war injuries just a few years ago. You can see how much it would have meant to me to have Armand come home. Jean's widow, Michele, lives here with her daughter Theresa, your first cousin. A distant cousin, Caron Laurens, came here after Jean's death to handle the marketing end of the business. Your father may have told you that I have never had a business head; it was Jean's sales ability that built up our trade. With Pierre's help, I still care for the vineyards.

"If it is possible, your mother's relatives, the Weills from across the river in Freiburg, will be here for your father's services. They are Frederich, Louis and Elsa—who was named for your mother. They are her brother Roderick's children, orphans now."

I sat back. My grandfather must be very old. My father was 57 when he died . . .

The train gave a skidding lurch and came to a shuddering halt which threw me forward and into the empty seat across the aisle. Instantly, Michael slid open the glass door. Even in my confusion, I knew he had been standing guard.

He dropped into the seat beside me and reached for the letter I had dropped. "Are you all right?"

When I had assured him that I was, he stood hesitantly in the doorway. "I'll try to find out what has happened. We're running late now."

His eyes were pinched with worry. I hoped that he wouldn't worry abut all of his patients in this way.

I looked at my watch. Our Rhine ship sailed at 5 a.m., but it would be terrible if I missed it. Father's casket would be aboard.

Moving to the window, I placed my cupped hands on the glass. There were no lights flickering beyond the patterned reflection of the train lights.

Michael came back almost immediately. "There's a washout and a freight stalled ahead. There will be a delay."

Our train began backing slowly as the conductor came in for our passports. Michael stepped into the aisle. He had gone pale. When he saw me looking in his passport, which was also green but a different shade, he gave me a wan smile. His worried eyes had an agonized expression. Something inside me wailed a silent question, "Michael, what are you hiding?"

I knew he was befriending me because I needed someone at this time. I had never been suspicious in my life; it was of course the knife in his pocket back on that bench on the quay that made me uneasy.

Still, my exhaustion and nerve strain made me sleep the rest of the way to Rotterdam with my head on his shoulder.

We arrived in a deluge of rain. Michael rushed me through the station and outside to a taxi. I had hoped to see the city, but our driver took a short route to our pier.

CHAPTER 4

As our taxi driver moved into line behind the other cabs, I wiped moisture from the window. Nothing father had told me prepared me for the cruise ship. With every window lighted, and strings of lights end to end, it loomed up out of the rain like a gigantic ocean liner in festive mood—far from my own mental state. I had begun to worry that the storm might have delayed the freighter. I had to know that the transfer had been made before I boarded.

A bright colored canopy covered the gangway. As each taxi moved forward it was met by uniformed boys holding large umbrellas. Luggage was swiftly removed by another team of boys and carried aboard.

I turned to Michael. "I must find out. I won't go if the freighter has been delayed."

"Certainly not. Run ahead and inquire. I'll see to your bags and meet you aboard."

As I stepped from the taxi and darted under the canopy, a tall and extremely handsome young man who had been scanning the arriving passengers, started down the gangway toward me.

He reached for the cosmetic bag I carried. "Daphne Laurens?" he asked me. His English was precise like

Michael's but with a slight accent. I presumed he was an officer of the ship.

"Yes. Has my father's . . .?"

"All has been taken care of, Daphne. As soon as the other late arriving passengers are dispersed, I shall take you there."

"Thank you." I turned to tell Michael who was paying the driver.

Michael looked up as a boy with bags passed me. I saw what I thought was a look of shock on Michael's always concerned face.

The man took my arm and turned me up the gangway. We were shoved along by stewards and other passengers. "I am your cousin Pierre Lilliard. Grandfather wrote to you in Paris that I would meet you here. He could not allow you to make this journey alone."

I turned my head to see if Michael was coming. He was gone. Another taxi had passed into the space and two couples were alighting.

Assuming that Michael had gone up the gangway and I had not seen him, I looked at the people gathered in the corridor. Some were passengers from our train. Michael was not among them.

An attractive girl in uniform was explaining that due to the inclement weather and the late arrival of many of the passengers, the buffet had been refashioned and now awaited the passengers in the dining salon. Would we please all go there while the luggage was placed in our staterooms?

It was not until Pierre was helping me out of my London Fog that I actually looked at him. There was in his attitude and carriage a positively regal bearing. His blonde hair was full and attractively cut to set off his well-formed face with wide set blue-grey eyes that were startlingly brilliant in the deep suntan of his skin. His dark suit was well cut. Even as he smiled down at me, I was aware of a cold sternness in his handsome face, and a sardonic twist in his smile. Had he not been so gentle and soft spoken, I should have been repelled.

I looked around the salon hoping to find Michael.

Pierre's eyebrows rose in a way I was to see many times. "Are you looking for someone? A passenger from your train? Or has a friend traveled with you after all?"

This taunting attitude was new to me. And it was very upsetting since I could think of no excuse for it. We were strangers meeting under difficult circumstances. It occured to me then that he had not wanted to meet me, but had done so to please grandfather.

"Yes, a student from Boston who is studying at Heidelberg. We rode out in the same taxi. He . . ."

"He has probably gone to his stateroom and you will see him in the morning. Come, let me fill a plate for you. The buffet is usually closed much earlier and I suspect the crew would be glad to clear up here. Will you have wine or coffee?"

With a courtesy I had loved in my father and admired in most of the French since I had come to Europe, he led me to the long table that displayed an elaborate array of sea foods, sliced ham, turkey, pate, small round tomatoes, and delectable huge strawberries. I was standing in front of a tray of assorted sweet rolls. Picking up a small saucer, I chose two. Again I received the raised eyebrow that made me feel like a child who had done something wrong.

He led me to a table beside the window. "Tomorrow, tables will be assigned which passengers will use throughout the trip. I have told the steward that we shall want this one."

Nothing more was needed to tell me that Pierre

Lilliard was accustomed to giving orders and being obeyed. The table was set for two. And what about Michael who had befriended me, and who was aboard this ship because of me . . .?

Pierre, who had eaten earlier, sat sipping wine and studying me. I was most uncomfortable under his scrutiny.

"Thank you for making sure that . . ."

"There was more to it than merely checking. Cruise ships do not carry cargo. Fortunately, we have business connections. This has been done as a favor. I took the stateroom that was to have been your father's. A crew member's cabin was selected. At the time the arrangements were made the ship was sold out. Now the weather has brought cancellations."

His choice of words was deplorable to me. "I'm sorry. I should have made other arrangements."

"I think these were not your arrangements, but were your grandfather's. You will find him a sentimental man who loved his sons deeply."

"And carrying out grandfather's wishes has been an embarrassment to you. I am very sorry."

I started to rise. He put out a hand to stop me. "Please finish your meal. I did not want to upset you."

It was not until after the other passengers had gone to their staterooms that Pierre led me below. Father's casket, now encased in a metal carrier, had been placed on a lowered bunk. Someone had thoughtfully carried one of the attractive floral arrangements from the dining salon and placed it on a small table.

As I sat down on a chair that had been placed next to the bunk, Pierre went out and closed the door. I rested my head against the cold metal. How differently we were traveling than we had planned. But, his ship had not been delayed. We were coming at last to the end of a journey that should have been made many years earlier.

I stood up resolutely. At Chateau Laurens I would find out what had happened those long years ago that would keep father and grandfather separated after mother was gone. I knew now that there had been a deep love between the two men. I hoped that I, Elsa's daughter, had not been the instrument of their agony. If this had been so, father would not have been so elated when grandfather's welcoming letter had come. Or, perhaps that had been his worry. How terribly he must have wanted to go home . . .

Before opening the door, I gave my eyes a final swipe.

Pierre, who had waited outside, closed and locked the door and gave the key to me. Tucking my arm under his, he led me up the stairs. We turned to the right, down the corridor. I had never been on a ship. It was like a hotel.

Pierre stopped in front of a door. "We'll have a drink in my cabin, then you should retire. You look exhausted. I'm sure this has been a hard trip for you. I told your grandfather that it would be far easier for you to fly to Strasbourg and do your sightseeing under less strain, but as I told you, he is a sentimental man."

I was certain that Pierre was not sentimental, that nothing could penetrate his hard exterior. It surprised me that grandfather had been able to influence Pierre to carry out his wishes.

His stateroom was so delightful that I exclaimed, "How very lovely."

"Your accommodations are the same."

A ship's whistle sounded outside. He walked swiftly to the window and raised the shade and beckoned to me to join his as a large lighted ship passed slowly. I was fascinated. As our ship rolled in the wake of the passing ship, the movement pushed me against Pierre who reached out to steady me. To my surprise and in spite of my irritation at his manner I wanted to lean against him, bury my face in his expensive suit and cry.

There were ships and small lighters, similar to the Bateau Mouche of Paris, moving in the harbor, their lights eerily misty in the rain. I stood watching them while Pierre opened a tan valise which held bottles of wine and glasses. When he drew out a bottle I recognized the label. This was the same Reisling Michael had ordered in Paris, but of a different vintage.

At the thought of Michael, I shivered. What could have happened to him? He must surely be aboard. Perhaps he had assumed as I had that Pierre was a ship's representative greeting me and thought that I might prefer being alone with him at that time.

We sat sipping the wine. Perhaps Michael, with his quick mind, had assumed, and rightly, that someone had come from Strasbourg to meet me, and decided to cancel the slower trip by river and take the train to Heidelberg. It seemed unlikely that he would go without telling me since he could have had any one of the many cabs that left the dock empty.

When I saw Pierre looking at me, I forced myself to smile at him. "It was lovely of you to meet me, and to come so well prepared. The wine is delicious."

"Your grandfather sent it. He knew your grief and thought this might ease it. I wanted very much to come since he could not."

"He isn't ill."

"He's had two shocks, first, that his son was alive, then worse, to have him die before he could come home. Also, he is too old to be working as hard as he is."

"Times are hard with today's high prices. I should imagine he feels that he must work hard."

Pierre put down his glass and his eyebrows rose in that sardonic way. His head tilted slightly as he continued to look at me. "So you think your grandfather has financial problems."

It was such a strange remark, and so sarcastically toned that I was astonished. My eyes, heavy with unshed tears, blinked.

"I have no idea of my grandfather's financial affairs."

"But I'm sure you are most interested. Within a few days you will be well informed. I take it that you did not receive his last letter. No matter. It will be forwarded. I presume you left a forwarding address."

He sounded as if he knew what grandfather had written. "You mean that I did not know you would meet me? Yes, the letter came to the Choiseul. I was on my way to the American Express office and put it in this passport slot of my purse. There was an accident."

His eyes flew open; he had been examining me under almost closed lids. "What do you mean?" he snapped sharply.

"There was a crowd at the mail window. It was closing time. When I turned in the crowd to leave, my umbrella caught someone's arm. My arm rammed something sharp." I pushed up my jacket sleeve to show him the bandage, feeling extremely young and foolish. Yet I felt that I had to explain losing grandfather's letter.

"The young man I have been looking for aboard saw the blood and took me upstairs to the nurse. Michael kept insisting that had I not swerved, the knife would have gone into my back. He was sure it was intentional.

I knew that could not be. If anyone had wanted to steal my purse, it would have been easy to do with no reason for stabbing me."

He sat so absolutely still that not one muscle of his body moved, nor did one in his face. His eyes never left mine, nor did they change expression.

"If this Michael was so certain someone tried to stab you, why didn't he have the manager lock the door and call the police? Or why didn't the nurse?"

"I assured them that I knew no one in Paris and that no one had any reason to want to kill me. But it was unnerving."

"I should imagine so." His expression was inscrutable. "Then I presume this young man befriended you."

"Michael Strange from Boston, a student at Heidelberg. Yes, he went back to the hotel with me."

"To look after a fellow American in a strange land." There was no doubting the taunting in his tone. I wondered why he would hate me. Certainly no one was sarcastic to a stranger for no reason.

I stood up, suddenly desperately tired. "I should like to go to my stateroom now."

He was on his feet instantly and looking down at me with a gentleness I could not believe. In my weak-minded condition, this devastatingly handsome man disturbed me more than I wanted to admit. I fervently hoped that when we reached Chateau Laurens he would get into his coveralls or whatever he wore to work in the vineyards and never again cross my path.

As he led me to the door, he leaned down and pressed my shoulders. "I, for one, am exceedingly glad this supposed killer did not succeed." He picked up the wine bottle as we left his stateroom.

In my stateroom he switched on the lights. Removing a carafe of water from the wall bracket, he placed the wine bottle there.

"Have a small glass when you are ready to retire. That will take away bad dreams. The ship will rock you into the healing arms of sleep."

I stared at him. Perhaps he was drunk. He seemed like a man who was unused to gentleness and pleasantries but determined to accomplish both. I was far too weary to worry about Pierre Lilliard tonight, or rather, this morning. I wanted absolutely nothing to do with a handsome stranger whose fast changing moods could upset me so terribly.

I held out my hand. "Thank you for your graciousness in meeting me." I was being sarcastic now. There had been little graciousness. He had managed to make me feel younger than my twenty years, unsophisticated, yes, and even shabby in my hand-made suit. No one had ever done that to me in my life.

"You should sleep in. I've ordered a light breakfast to be served in your room. There will be the Captain's reception in the main salon at eleven. I shall come for you."

"I shouldn't like attending a party, thank you very much however."

Once again I saw the firming of his jawline and the stern expression return to those attractive grey blue eyes.

"I should attend if I were you. There will be a good explanatory lesson on your trip up the Rhine, given in English as well as other languages. Excellent light sandwiches and beverages will be served."

We had been speaking English, and his was perfect, probably university taught, more formal than mine.

Some inner feeling that was like a warning, which I was to find greatly to my advantage, made me decide not to tell Pierre that I understood French better than I spoke it.

As he bowed from the corridor, I turned the key in the lock. Sitting on the bed which was open and ready, I gazed out the window at the distant lights on shore glittering on the wet pane. I was shaking. No one had ever upset me so much. One minute I wanted consolation in his evident strength, and the next minute I had the wildest desire to slap him. An enigma. And he would remain one to me for some time to come.

I did as he suggested. When I had unpacked my nightrobe, and prepared for bed, I poured a small amount of the light wine into a glass and sipped it . . .

All the days since I left home, and especially in the nights, my mind had kept saying, "I'm never going to see my father again." Now that sober refrain kept repeating. Within a few days he would be buried in his own family graveyard. I would go back to Taos with only one grave to tend.

Even though it had been my father's wish and my grandfather's, I wanted to be home among friends and familiar things. I was sorry I had made this trip. I was going to be more than sorry . . .

CHAPTER 5

A note on ship's stationary arrived on my tray with coffee and croissants. I snatched it eagerly knowing that it would be from Michael. I much preferred Michael's worried countenance to the arrogance of Pierre Lilliard. But it was not Michael's handwriting. This handwriting was tall and firm, each letter perfectly formed and lacked the informality of my grandfather's handwriting.

"Daphne: I should appreciate your attending the Captain's reception. I shall be at your door at five minutes to eleven. Be prompt."

I had already decided to attend. Father would want me to learn all that I could about his beloved Rhine River.

While I sipped my coffee, I read the colorful folder that had been placed on my table near the window. The first day aboard we would travel along the Waal, an arm of the Rhine, as far as the Dutch-German border near Emmerich. Reaching over, I raised the shade of my large picture window.

A light rain still fell. A delightful small bateau came floating past. Two small children bundled up in heavy sweaters and snug knitted caps with huge pompoms played with a small dog on the fore deck. A woman with a scarf flying from her head and a huge apron tied around her was hanging children's clothing on a line that had been stretched the length of the ship. Potted geraniums of vivid red lined the decks. It was evident the boat was the family home as well as the husband's business of carrying cargo.

With the help of a long folded map I tried to find our location. My watch had stopped and I had not yet unpacked my small travel clock, but I knew we'd been moving for many hours. In half-sleep, I had been aware of chains dropping and the slam of a great door that I knew must be where I entered the ship. I had heard whistles and bells, but I had not wanted to wake up to face reality.

Finally, I decided I should dress so as to be ready promptly at five minutes to eleven. By now I knew that I was not going to please Pierre. I was going to the reception to search for Michael.

Brushing didn't help the black suit I had traveled in the day before, but I supposed that other travelers would have the same problems of wrinkles after the heavy downpour. I chose a white blouse with collar and cuffs trimmed with a fine lace I'd found in mother's trunk.

The mirror was discouraging. My eyes, which are black on dull days, were deeply circled. I applied makeup which I hoped covered the circles, put on the soft pink lipstick a girl in Sante Fe had assured me was becoming with my tan, and pulled on the black kid gloves I'd bought in Paris.

As I stepped into the corridor, Pierre, stunning in a tweed suit, strode toward me.

"Good morning, Daphne. You look refreshed, and very beautiful. Last night I thought you were pretty, but I see that was an understatement."

"Thank you."

Passengers were gathered in the salon, a huge room tastefully furnished with divans, tables, and chairs that swiveled to give views from the large picture windows on each side.

We were led to one of the tables overlooking the prow allowing the best possible view. It was evident that Pierre had made arrangements for such good seats since the room was full.

The Captain explained various views along the Rhine route which would be announced over the speaking system in time for passengers to have cameras at the ready. We were told, in four languages, that since nothing could be done about the weather the ship's officers and crew would make up for the rain by giving excellent service and entertainment.

As we entered and walked through the salon, I had scanned faces looking for Michael. When the trays of sandwiches and cups of hot boullion were carried in, I took the opportunity to look again. Michael was not in the salon.

We were traveling through Dutch countryside with the canals and dikes running through the meadows. Now and then, I glimpsed a large windmill and a scene of a pleasant and colorful farm would emerge from the gloom. Numerous passengers rushed out to photograph them from the sliding doors.

I had traveled my own beautiful and varied country with father on his painting trips so that I had seen our wide rivers. We had both loved travel features on television, so that I had seen something of the world, but those views did not compare with the exciting and exotic scenes of the old world passing on either side of the river. The architecture of the buildings and houses was entirely different from any I had seen.

It was during luncheon that we made a brief stop at Emmerich, a village of tall, handsome, old houses placed close to the quay. Far up the quay and led by a guide who was gesturing, were more than a hundred old gentlemen in dark suits and overcoats, a few with umbrellas.

Pierre saw me looking at them. "Those gentlemen are retirees being treated by Holland to this trip up the Rhine. Many cruise ships that we shall pass are carrying retirees and invalids for the first trip of their lives."

He kept watching me for my reactions which I could not and did not try to suppress. I was thrilled with the number of boats and ships traveling the Rhine, certainly many ships bigger than some that ply the oceans of the world.

It was the little ones that I called "house-business boats" that delighted me most. There were huge freighters and vessels not self-propelled, but towed. Many barges were fastened together and towed by tugs. As we came into view, the skippers determined passage safety with whistles that indicated their sailing directions.

Pierre explained the various signals and the tugs. "The tug has no cargo except very high horsepowered engines, and crews who live aboard. If you spot a yellow cylinder on a first barge, you can expect quite a few barges are following."

At that moment the excited voice on the speaking system announced that the most powerful tug on the Rhine, the *Unterwalden*, a Swiss vessel of 4000 horsepower, was coming into view. Many passengers scurried around with cameras.

The barges were immense and covered with cargo evenly packed so as not to be top-heavy.

That had no sooner passed than we were passed by a fast vessel going in the same direction which Pierre explained was a self-propelled freighter. This particular one with a large F carried inflammable cargo and was called a motor tanker. A small boat came into view towing a tremenous barge. On it were more of the delightful children.

"Those children look school age. If they spend their lives on the barges, how do they get an education?"

"In all of the larger Rhine ports are special schools and homes for river children. On holidays and weekends, the family picks up the children. They love the exciting life and often know no other. Some boats have been in the family for generations. Also, along the Rhine, are training ships where cabin boys learn the trade. These are anchored at various ports as are schools of navigation. Mighty important on a busy river of this size."

"It's a little world in itself."

"Far more than that. Much of the industrial and the agricultural products are shipped up and down river rather than carried overland."

We returned to the salon where once again I swept the faces of passengers hoping to find Michael. Had something happened to him? Could the man who had obviously been following me that last day in Paris have been hoping that I would lead him to Michael? Perhaps the knife had been meant for him, and he knew it. That could have been Michael's reason for making the excursion through the long train. I felt sure that if anything had happened at the boat landing in Rotterdam I should have heard about it by now.

Pierre touched my arm. "I've been giving you a lesson in navigation. You aren't listening." The reproach in his voice was unmistakable. Turning, I saw again his disapproval of me.

"I'm sorry." I watched two of the swift trains that ran along the riverbank pass. I knew Pierre's expression could be the normal one of an unpleasant person, but Pierre had proven himself to be a warm companion and an understanding one. I supposed that his problem was me, that this trip and I were nuisances. But if he considered me a nuisance, why did he stare at me so hard? Sometimes when he looked at me his eyes twinkled as if he held some secret concerning me. I wouldn't let myself think that a man of his worldliness and extreme good looks could entertain any desires toward a girl as small and plain as I. Now he was looking at me in total disapproval.

"What are you thinking?"

"I've been worrying about Michael. I'm afraid something has happened to him. He might be ill in his stateroom," Or dead. That thought had occurred to me more than one.

"How did it happen that this young man had reservations on the same ship as you did? Isn't that too much of a coincidence?" He frowned. "Why should you worry about a stranger you encountered in Paris, someone you shall never see again? Certainly if anything had happened aboard, we would have heard about it."

I decided to tell him everything. "Michael was so certain that someone had tried to kill me that he felt I needed someone to look after me on the trip. Because of cancellations, he was able to make a reservation."

"When exactly did you see him last?"

"When you met me on the gangway. He was paying the taxi driver."

"Then isn't it logical to assume that he saw that you were properly met and would be supervised, and decided to proceed to Heidelberg by a faster route? However, so that you will be better able to enjoy your trip, I shall go to the purser and inquire if he did fill his reservation aboard ship. His name again, if you please."

"Michael Strange of Boston. I shall go with you."

"That is not necessary. There is some beautiful scenery coming into view which you wouldn't want to miss. I shall report back to you."

The scenery was exciting now. Passengers were leaping around chairs with cameras. Boys outside on deck were wiping the drenched windows with long handled wipers which didn't do much good. The rain was torrential. On the left bank I did glimpse a small hamlet with roofs of delicate coloring and steeples and what appeared to be old Roman walls. I had not been listening to the announcements.

Pierre did not return immediately, and I worried, but not about him. It was a relief that he was not at my side to either stare or give me disparaging glances.

As rain teemed, and passengers were restless, I decided to go to my stateroom. I could be alone and could watch the scenery on one side of the ship.

CHAPTER 6

I lay with a robe covering me watching a tremendous industrial area with miles of wharf districts. Factory fumes and smoke wavered up into the sheets of rain.

By tea-time I returned to the salon. Pierre sat reading, and got up when I approached.

"Evidently you were not as anxious about your friend as you let me believe."

No one had ever spoken to me as contemptuously in my life. I found the experience quite shocking.

"Your friend Michael Strange did not make a reservation aboard this ship."

I sat down. I did not believe him. I told myself that I would go to the purser at some convenient time since it would not be polite to admit my disbelief to this man who was so close to my grandfather. The more I saw of Pierre, the less I could imagine him with his sleeves rolled up working in the vineyards with grandfather.

He picked up his book and resumed reading. I sat contemplating his words. Michael had seemed happy to get his reservation; he was going to show me the river, and tell me the history as he had done on our short excursion in Paris. I felt wounded if he had lied. But why should he?

I shook my head. Michael would not lie. However briefly I had known him, I knew his qualities. He was going to become a doctor to help his sister. He was fine and good. Above all, he would not have left without telling me his plans had changed. He could easily have found me by walking into the dining salon.

It must have been that upon seeing Pierre greet me, he decided instantly that I was going to travel with someone from Chateau Laurens, and that he could therefore get along with his own life. But I honestly didn't believe that.

Pierre roused himself from his book for tea, and assumed his gracious attitude. When he was like that he was charming.

Some time later, I noticed the ladies slipping away, presumably to dress for dinner. I had packed long dresses and cocktail dresses in the bag that held my father's paintings. I had not unpacked that bag at home although it seemed unlikely that I would need the dresses at my grandfather's home.

Now, I felt that I would like to have Pierre see me in a particular green dress that I had made of one of the new soft materials that were flattering to my small figure. Excusing myself, I went to my stateroom.

Dragging the heavy bag from the large closet, I placed it on the floor and unlocked it. In spite of packing the green dress in a plastic bag, I found it hopelessly wrinkled. That left a choice of a slim-line black gown with gold trim of brocade I'd found in mother's trunk. The dress had been the dream of my life. Father and I attended a few social functions and those were very informal. I would almost always go in a sweater and skirt. Evenings in Taos were cool, and in winter often exceedingly cold with snow.

I had seen the dress in one of the better Santa Fe shops where a friend worked. I couldn't afford it, but we had taken it into the fitting room where I tried it on. Afterward, she brought a sheaf of tissue paper and scissors. I made a pattern, bought material and made the dress. When I was going through mother's trunk for lace for the blouse I was wearing, I had seen the brocade, and decided to insert it from the underarm down each side and to add an Oriental collar. I'd put in a zipper from the neck to below my waist to allow an easy entry into a dress that was too slim to have enough give to pull it over my head. When finished, it did not look like the dress in Santa Fe, but had the same severe and flattering lines.

I couldn't stop my tears when I hung up the last of the dresses. Father had been delighted over my "design." Mother had made her dresses and suits. He had gone to the closet they had shared and from far to the back drew out a hanging bag containing clothing she had made for a life more social than ours. All of the lovely creations fit me with a bit of alterations. They were an odd length. Father told me wartime dresses were referred to as having "The New Look." It came halfway between the knees and the ankle and must have sent women into the depths of despair. It was unbecoming.

One cocktail dress, of beautiful French brocade, was sleeveless, form-fitting with short pleats on each side and front where she had placed delicate satin bows. Now, standing in front of the full length door mirror, I tried it on. I had shortened it. I dug out a pair of black satin slippers. My decision was made.

After my bath, I opened the Shalimar perfume that I had bought in Paris. That had been on my first day when I wandered up the Rue de la Paix and was thrilled to find a Guerlain shop in my neighborhood. It had been an extravagant gesture.

Pierre had asked me to come to his stateroom for a glass of grandfather's Reisling before dinner. Gathering up my black wool shawl, I went down the corridor and tapped on his door

Opening it, he took a deep breath and sighed. "Shalimar. My favorite of all women's perfumes. And it is right for you, Daphne."

He closed the door and stood looking down at me. "I'm going to have to stop thinking of you as a little girl."

I decided he had been nipping at the wine.

"How old are you, Daphne?" Picking up the wine bottle, he filled two glasses.

"I'm twenty. Mother was thirty-five when I was born."

He was studying my dress, making me self-conscious because it was so old. "You went shopping in Paris."

My heart sang. "Not for dresses, just for a few small luxuries. Mother made this during the war from material she brought from France." Father had told me she bought it for her trousseau, never dreaming that the shadows of war would soon close over them to send them across thousasnds of miles to a new life.

He sipped his wine. "Strange, that your parents never wrote to their families. Believe me, Daphne, your first letter so happily read by your grandfather just about put the rest of the family into shock."

He was trying to tell me something, trying to warn me—I was to learn later in terror and despair.

"I never knew we had relatives until father's illness. I

found grandfather's name and address in his safety deposit box."

He nodded thoughtfully and changed the subject abruptly. "You must be the same size as your mother . . ."

"Not exactly. I had to let out the side seams and shorten this one." I was suddenly happy I had brought the gowns.

He laughed. "Well, it is lovely, but you tell too much. Had you told me you bought this one in Paris, I would have believed it. You should keep this sort of thing to yourself."

"In my country it is considered economical to make one's own clothing. I made the black suit I wore yesterday and the blouse. The lace came from mother's trunk."

His hands fanned out in mock despair. "What a child you are. So innocent of worldly ways. Some women would stitch a Paris label inside to hide the fact that an article is handmade."

"In our country one can order labels with one's own name to prove one made a costume."

"Your grandfather is going to love you. Your cousin Theresa will loathe you."

"No. She is the one I have looked forward to meeting. Why should she hate me?"

He lowered his glass. His face was so serious that I thought he was going to tell me more than he did. I could see him change his mind as his expression changed with it.

"You are much prettier than she is, warmer, and, I am supposing, kind. Also, you are talented and self-sufficient. Theresa is . . . I shall let you find out for yourself, but do be warned."

He said those last words with so much emphasis, so much foreboding that a chill passed through me. I pulled my shawl around my shoulders.

I watched his struggle. There were dark days ahead for me. Pierre wanted me to know in advance that besides my grief I had other problems to face.

He placed his hands on my shoulders. "Daphne, I have been testing you this far on the trip. I have found you too sensitive, too vulnerable. As much as I should like to, I won't be around all of the time to ward off hurts . . . Now, we shall stop being serious. We'll be stopping for the night in Dusseldorf. You have a choice of a night tour by bus, or coming ashore with me while I make a telephone call. If you don't mind walking in the rain, some of the shops remain open late for tourists who wish to see the wares, and to buy them, of course."

"I'd love to go with you. I've always wanted to see Germany, especially the Black Forest." I could never tell Pierre how much I longed to do that. In mother's trunk I had found a battered but lovely little house, delicately and intricately carved of wood. A thermometer, a little more than an inch tall under the roof, and charming little dolls, a man and woman who came forward to forecast the weather, stood under latticed windows and window boxes with red geraniums. On each side of the porch were perfectly carved pine trees. I had been a small child when father carried mother's trunk to my room. The little house and a worn doll were the first treasures from it. I still had them both. How childish Pierre would think I was if he knew.

"You shall one day." He seemed so certain, and sat nodding his head studying me. "Yes, you shall see the Black Forest."

"That is unlikely. After father's funeral I must get

back to my shop. I turned it over to a friend to run while father and I . . ."

"But you and your father planned to be away for months. If this friend promised at an earlier time to stay, why can't she do just that after you write that your grandfather wants to keep you for a long visit?"

"He may not. He may not have room for me. He wrote about so many who live with him."

Pierre let his head drop back while he laughed, then he glanced at his watch.

"We shall see. Let's go to dinner."

After dinner we strolled into the main salon where musicians were playing Lara's Theme from "Dr. Zhivago," that haunting "Somewhere, My Love."

As if it had been preplanned, Pierre swept me into his arms, and we danced. I was surprised that such a large man was so light on his feet. Father had been a good dancer. We often danced to records on the hifi set he built.

"You are not smiling, Daphne."

No, I was not smiling. I was on the verge of tears. Father and I had seen "Dr. Zhivago" three times and each time father sat in some far distant dream of his own. He had bought four different arrangements of Lara's Theme, and during the long days of his illness, had played it almost constantly.

As the words of the song passed through my mind I knew why my father had listened to it so often. In a moment of inexplicable horror, I realized that I had left mother alone in that place so far from her homeland. I should have brought her home with father. This sent me into deeper despair.

But as the musicians swept into a cheerful polka, we danced until I was breathless and laughing.

Afterward, Pierre held me off and looked down at me. "Someone has taught you to polka, and very well."

"Father. We often danced."

"What a remarkable child you are turning out to be. I had expected to be escorting a wailing child, instead I find a charming companion. If I had guessed, I shouldn't have made further arrangements that I did make. I'm afraid I'm going to regret it."

I was not to know what further arrangements he had made until our stop at Koblenz and I was not going to like them.

With my arm tucked in his, we walked to the windows. Rain still fell.

"You'd better change into something warmer and that charming raincoat you wore as you boarded ship. We're almost to Dusseldorf."

"I hope I can find a Black Forest cuckoo clock. I'm so glad we are stopping in a German city. I've wanted a real one all of my life."

"A cuckoo clock?" He stopped in the middle of the stairway blocking passengers who were hurrying down to disembark. Taking my chin in his hands, he raised my face.

"Didn't your father tell you anything about his life in France? Didn't he tell you anything about his home?"

"Pierre, we're blocking the stairway."

I couldn't answer him until we reached my doorway. "He spoke of the countryside and of the Rhine. He painted scenes from his childhood." Our home was full of paintings that he had done of France.

He nodded. I liked him better tonight than I had

thought possible. He understood what it must be like to be an exile in a distant land and to feel that you could never come home. I was grateful for that moment. As if to seal the understanding that had passed between us, he bent and touched my lips with his. Then he turned quickly and stroke down the corridor.

I stepped inside, oddly shaken. I knew that I had better get through with my ordeal and go home. There would be no time for me to travel to the Black Forest. I would find and buy my cuckoo clock tonight . . .

I changed to a warm sweater and skirt, boots and raincoat, and carried my umbrella.

When I reached the gangway, the disembarking passengers and their luggage were gone. Pierre stood leaning against the wall, smoking a cigarette. He didn't see me; he was lost in thought.

"Pierre, I'm ready." Without a word, he took my umbrella and opened it.

From the moment we walked from the gangway into the tree lined quay I became conscious of footsteps behind us. Twice I looked back and saw no one, but the streets were dark and full of shadows. We passed through a dimly lit warehouse district where the sounds behind us seemed to echo. Seeing no one, I assumed I had been hearing the echo of our footsteps.

The lights of the city, diffused by rain, reflected eerily upon the streets and dark buildings giving the town an air of mystery.

Soon we came upon a narrow, brightly lighted street. Pierre pointed out an appealing looking shop where other passengers already mingled among tables and shelves of china. "You'll find what you want here, Daphne. Don't leave the store until I come back. I shouldn't be very long."

Facing a wall of cuckoo clocks, I forgot my apprehension caused by the footsteps. Fascinated, I walked up and down until I saw my clock, a hunter's clock, a wooden house similar to mother's little one. A six-antlered deer was mounted upon a seal on the roof above crossed muskets. The hunter's horn wrapped the face of the clock. On one side hung a rabbit; on the other a pheasant with a saddle bag beneath.

I told a woman I would buy it. As I counted out traveler's checks, I was mentally hanging it at home. Sadly, I knew that once my mission in Strasbourg was accomplished, I would go back and try to fit into a semblance of my old life.

I had been so busy with my shop, and in the past two years nursing father, that I had not had time to concentrate on any of my friends. Although Pierre had been gone only a short time, I felt lost without him. This would not do. I knew that. We were worlds apart . . .

At that moment and with a delightful cacophony of sound, all of the clocks began to strike the hour of nine, to sound out with bells, music, strident striking and bonging. I stood listening. Unexpectedly but inexorably came that chilling feeling of doom, as if the striking of the clocks told a warning. I stood, hands iced, waiting for my package. Other shoppers were leaving the store. Pierre had not come back.

CHAPTER 7

An elderly man, in a dark blue apron with a key ring hanging from a worn leather belt at his waist, smiled at me and unlocked the door.

Outside stood a man in a black raincoat such as Pierre had worn. With a great relief, I moved forward. Light from the store behind me flashed upon metal as a knife was thrust toward me. The old gentlemen flung out his hands pitching me forward to the stone sidewalk. He called out to the woman still in the shop. The woman grabbed at my coat and tugged me back inside. The old man bustled after my attacker to give chase.

"Don't let him," I cried out in French which she understood. "He might be killed."

The quick action of that old man had saved my life. There was no question in my mind now. That was the same man who had followed me in Paris, the same one who had attempted to stab me in the American Express office where I had spoken my name clearly. And where my grandfather's letter had been lost. Someone was determined that I not reach Chateau Laurens alive. But for what reason?

While I stood trembling, the woman in the shop had been speaking to me.

"Don't worry about Gustave. He is very capable and has foiled more than one holdup. I'm sorry that it happened to you. Your face. Your coat. Your knees . . ."

Stunned, my mind whirled. At home I should have immediately called the police to tell them an attempt had been made on my life and that an instant search of the area might locate the killer. Here in this strange country, I did not know what to do. Many men wore black raincoats. As on the other two occasions, I had not been able to grasp any particular characteristic of the man except at American Express and on the Place de la Concorde I had seen the cruel eyes. Now at this distance I wondered if I had even imagined that those two men were the same. Many persons were nondescript, were able to pass unnoticed through any crowd.

Yet someone wanted to kill me. In horror, I followed the woman's hands pointing out the damages of my hard and sudden crash to the sidewalk.

Although I was coming out of my shock, I still trembled uncontrollably. My hand went up to my cheek as recognition of pain came suddenly.

"Yes, your cheekbone might be cracked, and the skin is grazed." The woman pulled toward me a small gold chair and eased me into it. As she walked behind the counter, she kept looking back to make sure I would not fall over.

I glanced down at my knees. I'd landed hard on them. My stockings were torn and muddy, but my knees were merely scraped. My coat was soaked with the muddy water on the sidewalk.

She came back with a bottle of alcohol and cotton and began cleaning my cheek. I rolled down my stockings while she swiped at my knees. I almost fainted as a key turned in the lock. The old man came in carrying my package which evidently I had dropped and forgotten. He spoke to the woman in German. We had been speaking in French.

"He says he is very sorry. The man got away. He will unpack and inspect your clock. If it hit the sidewalk as hard as you did, it will be broken and we will replace it with another." The old man spoke a long string of agonized words to me.

"He is trying to tell you that he reacted too quickly and is sorry that he shoved you so hard. He is deeply regretful of your injuries."

"Please tell him that he probably saved my life and that I am exceedingly grateful."

She drew back in horror. "Your life?"

The old man nodded vigorously.

"Then he had a gun. They usually do."

"I saw a knife."

She turned to the old man and questioned him sharply. He nodded again. Then I had not imagined it. The light had flashed on the blade, and it had been meant for me.

My clock was broken. The antlered deer had been crushed. It was like a dreadful omen to me. The old man brought out another like it and showed it to me. The woman hovered wringing her hands.

"You must not go back to your ship alone. I will call a taxi for you. Or if you wait, we will walk there with you. It is not safe to walk alone at night."

I explained that my cousin had gone to make a telephone call and would be back for me.

"Then you must wait inside with us while we pack the safe."

Bustling around under the counter, Gustave brought forth a large impressive looking pistol. Stooping again, he came up with a bottle of dark brandy and glasses. The liqueur which had an anise flavor was sickeningly sweet but it warmed me and had a soothing effect. I sat sipping it, holding it with both shaking hands while they went on with their business of placing money and travelers' checks and jewelry, all the time talking in German. I caught a few words: "Kopfschmerzen." They thought I would have a headache, or I was a headache to them. Father, teasing me, had used that word.

All of my life I had been in the habit of trying to talk myself out of things: our money worries in my younger years, my early shyness and introverted traits that I had begun to believe came from being a lonely child living with a gloomy father. I did it now while they covered counters and tables.

My imagination had always been vivid. In childhood I had imagined myself to be the daughter of royalty hidden in Taos for some mystical reason, or some political plan. Could I have been imagining that someone wanted to kill me? Then I did find a possible excuse. One does make efforts to draw away from distressing thoughts. I was being mistaken for someone else, someone I resembled . . . That was a logical idea and I clamped on to it.

The clocks began to ring and bong and announce the hour of nine-thirty. Where was Pierre? He would surely know that the shops closed at nine.

When the couple had put on raincoats and were ready to leave the shop, the woman came to me to re-examine my cheek.

"Tomorrow you will have what is called the purple

eye, I fear. Are you less frightened now? Would you like another brandy? No? Then we shall walk with you to the ship. Your cousin has been delayed, no doubt, and will expect you to return there."

Gustave picked up the heavy gun and placed it in his pocket.

My knees shook as I waited on the sidewalk with her while Gustave locked the door and turned the keyring and shoved it under his belt.

"Come with us, poor child. I feel it would be wise for you to have the doctor aboard look at your cheek, and perhaps give you a sedative. You are most unnerved and rightly so."

As we started across the street, Pierre came running from the shop door.

"Daphne, I am so sorry to have been delayed."

Gustave, who had stepped in front of us and brought out his pistol, placed it back in his pocket.

"This is my cousin," I said in English to the woman who looked at me strangely.

Pierre told her of his delay in French. The woman, still studying me curiously, told Pierre of the intended robbery and of my injuries and ordered him to make me see the doctor the instant we boarded ship. She was annoyed with him, and he recognized it and apologized. His wet face was white and strained.

After he had thanked them both, he took my wrist in a vise-like grip, and we started for the ship.

"Give me your package. This is your much desired cuckoo clock, I take it. Now, you tell me what happened. The shopkeeper said there had been an attempted robbery as you were leaving."

As we walked, I told him what had happened. I don't

know what made me keep from him my fear that the attacker had been the same one in Paris. The street lights were dim now, and the city so quiet under the soft rain that our footsteps echoed hollowly in the tunnel-like area where we walked between old buildings. The sounds brought back the memory of the other footsteps and I shuddered in a paroxysm of terror.

"You were frightened and hurt and all because I was determined to reach my party on long distance to cancel the other arrangements I had made. I was unable to reach my party. Before meeting you in Rotterdam it had seemed a good idea."

As we drew under a street lamp, he looked down into my face. "That's a nasty looking cheek. It has already begun to swell."

"Yes, I struck the sidewalk hard. The crash also broke my clock but the couple replaced it."

"You shall see the doctor the instant we get aboard. Evidently your being in the doorway interrupted a robbery of the shop."

"The old gentleman was unlocking the door for me to leave. They had already closed for the night."

It was not until we were walking down the corridor on the ship that he called my attention to a slit in my coat. It extended from my shoulder to my waist.

"I should have kept you with me. It appears that you are accident-prone. We shall have to take better care of you."

Two things were extremely interesting to me in the doctor's medicinal-smelling stateroom. Pierre, assuming as I had let him, that I did not understand French, told the doctor that I had fallen on a wet and slippery pavement. He did not mention the slit in my coat. He stood holding the wet and muddy coat folded in his arms while the doctor looked at my cheek.

"I told her she is accident-prone."

The doctor nodded and looked up at me as Pierre told him about the incident at American Express in Paris and asked him to look and to redress that wound also.

"Yes," the doctor spoke to me in English. "I am aware of your sad journey. It is quite true that grieving persons are often more accident-prone than normally. Roll up your sweater sleeve."

With considerable tut-tutting, he examined the wound and looked with question at Pierre.

Pierre glanced down sharply. "I did not notice how bad this was. You were not wearing the bandage early in the evening."

"I had covered it with a black velvet ribbon."

"Yes. I did notice that. It looked most attractive. I had presumed it was an American style bracelet."

As we parted at my door, Pierre handed me my umbrella and my package. He kept my coat folded. "This must go to be repaired and cleaned. I shall see to it. Try to rest. Since the doctor did not think you need take the sedative unless you are unable to sleep, I recommend a glass of your grandfather's wine. Rest well. Don't take both, Daphne. I'm deeply sorry about all of this."

Pierre's concerned expression remained with me as I prepared for bed.

Although I drank the wine, and drew my shade, I was still nervous. I got up twice to try the lock on my door and to make sure the slide-fastener was strong.

Through the turmoil of my mind my physical discomforts made themselves known. My knees ached. Evidently I had also pulled a muscle in my back. I did get the headache the shopkeeper had predicted, if that was a prediction and not an accusation. I finally fell into a troubled sleep aware of music floating down from the main salon where a dance must be in progress. Wafting into my subconscious came the strains of Lara's Theme, and the memory of dancing in Pierre's arms . . .

CHAPTER 8

I woke up the next morning to find our ship already in port in Cologne. At this stop we were docked right in the heart of the beautiful city. The rain had stopped momentarily and a bleak sun touched the spires of the magnificent cathedral and rooftops of the narrow four and five-story buildings lining the quay.

When my breakfast tray was delivered, I was handed a note from Pierre.

"Daphne: I hope that you are feeling well this morning. I shall be gone most of the day and will join the ship at five this evening at Koblenz. I suggest, if you are up to it, that you join other passengers on the sightseeing trip. Let us hope that your poor cheek is well, Pierre."

My poor cheek was not well. It waws grossly swollen, and, as predicted, discoloration had already begun around my eye. My elbow and both knees were sore. I was stiff and heartsick, and terribly, terribly lonely. And my disposition left much to be desired.

It was too late for me to join the sightseeing group. I dressed slowly, paying much attention to trying to cover my eye to finally decide that glasses, dark ones, would have to do. My raincoat had not been returned. After going out to the gangway, I discovered that the weather had turned very cold.

My only other heavy garment was a full-length black cape packed in the bottom of my large case that held father's paintings. It was too much of a chore to drag out the case in my condition and I was entirely too irritable to bother. It was as if my natural psychical sensitiveness was already predicting what lay ahead at Koblenz although at the moment my only thought of Koblenz was that was where I would see Pierre again.

Wearing my kneehigh leather boots, an added warm cardigan sweater and a large head scarf that concealed part of my cheek, I ventured down the gangway. I walked slowly up the tree-lined quay looking closely at the few people walking there. I wasn't going to be caught off guard again. I told myself that with the absence of my light tan coat, and with the concealing dark glasses and scarf, I would be hard to identify in a crowd. I joined a group alighting from another riverboat which proceeded, under brisk instruction from a tall and dictatorial woman guide, toward a string of waiting tour buses. I thought for a moment that I could board one of the buses and tour with them, but when I saw the guide demanding tickets from the tourists, I changed my mind and walked away.

Father had told me so much about the fabulous architecture of the most beautiful of gothic cathedrals that I was determined not to miss it on what would probably be my only trip to Europe. I walked slowly around it, gazing in awe at the dozens of intricately carved spires before I went inside. I entered with a tour group and was treated to a full and wondrous tour.

Since I planned to travel upriver to Koblenz, I took only a short walk around the city that was close to the quay. The few passengers who had remained on board had gathered for luncheon. Still wearing my disguise, I took a small table far from the one I usually shared with Pierre. I knew that I was probably being ridiculous to be so frightened. Near me passengers talked lightly of the dance on board tonight, and I hoped that my knees wouldn't be too stiff to prevent dancing with Pierre. As for my eye, which had darkened even more, I thought I could cover the area with makeup, or brazen it out. I wasn't the first person to have a black eye. As I dined, I planned exactly which dress I would wear, realizing that I was attempting to dazzle Pierre and at the same time recognizing that attempt as pitiful, considering what I had to work with.

After luncheon, I searched out the small cabin below. A fresh floral arrangement had been placed on the table. I sat for a long time staring out the window at the passing stream of navigation on the river. The ship was now underway. On shore, trains raced down the shining rails. There came the beginnings of steep slate-like mountains. We passed through an industrial area with towns but a few miles apart. A sign "Mondort" announced an old fishing port.

I got my guide book from my purse. We would soon come to the famed city of Bonn. I locked the door, and went to my cabin where I removed my outer sweater and scarf, then hurried up to the main salon. I chose a seat far from the one Pierre had had assigned to us.

Bonn was like so many we had passed, a combination of an ancient city blended with the new. Modern structures lined the riverbank. Flats. An old toll house. I was aware of the soft music coming over the sound system only when it was interrupted by the description of scenic views. Not more than a mile upriver was the industrial town of Beuel. From here on vineyards stretched up the mountains. Soil had been tilled until it seemed every inch of earth that was not rock had been set out in grapes. There came the first view of castles, some in ruins, that sent passengers scurrying outside with cameras.

The castles had been built on the tallest peaks. At the base of the mountains, some of the famous toll-houses still stood in their decay. There were islands in the river which made navigation extremely hazardous. I kept looking at my watch, anxious for Koblenz and Pierre's return.

Tea was served as we passed Remagen, a name I knew from the history of the war when in 1945, the first American troops marched across the bridge which the Germans had ordered blown up. Due to a misfire, the bridge had held up. Later, heavily damaged, it collapsed. Our guide told us the great piers had remained in the river until recently when they were removed. Twin towers still stood high on the banks.

In the sunlight reaching around regathering clouds, vineyards and castles brought gasps of delight from passengers.

When the ship finally slipped toward the dock at Koblenz, I saw Pierre's shining blonde head towering above the other waiting passengers. I rushed through the salon to greet him as he boarded.

When it seemed everyone must have passed me standing inside near the gangway, I moved out to look for him. He was coming up the middle of the gangway carrying a smart leather cosmetic case. His other arm grasped that of a tall and glamorous girl. He saw me, and with a bright smile, waved the case aloft. Placing the case in the hand of a waiting porter, he led the girl to my side.

She was his height in her heels, and in her feminine way, as stunningly handsome with her bright reddish blonde hair, her wide feline green-blue eyes, as water-pale as aquamarines. Add to that, natural long and thick black lashes that swept her cheeks as she glanced down at me while Pierre removed my dark glasses and examined my eye with a cluck of dismay.

"Nanette, this is my little cousin from America," he said in French. "Daphne Laurens," he said in English, "This is Mademoiselle Nanette Breton of Paris." Nanette smiled and nodded. Her attitude after a brief examination of me eliminated me as any possible adversary became almost friendly and she extended a long and graceful bejeweled hand.

In my old skirt and turtleneck sweater and boots, I barely came to her shoulder. After a few murmured words of sympathy to me which Pierre needlessly translated, she took his arm possessively.

"Really, Pierre, let us proceed to the salon for a drink. We can't go on blocking the passageway."

Her melodious voice and her beautiful French struck my ear with the impact of a fire siren. I stepped back, ready to go to my stateroom. Pierre snatched my elbow, the sore one, in a firm grip, and thrusting his arm through Nanette's, he steered us into the main salon where cocktails were flowing freely.

He leaned down to say to me: "I would much prefer that we have our glass of wine in my stateroom."

"What are you saying, Pierre?" Nanette asked sharply with a questioning glance down at me.

I would have much preferred going to my own stateroom and let my eye and my thoughts get darker and darker . . .

I sat primly sipping the wine Pierre had ordered for me, listening to the fast flow of French passing between them, secretly pleased that neither guessed I understood.

"The little pigeon is pretty. You didn't tell me. You kept referring to her as a little girl. I fully expected to be nursemaid to a wailing child. Naughty Pierre."

"I told you that you didn't need to come, that you could catch a train back to Paris, or extend your visit in Cologne."

"And miss the opportunity to offer my condolences to the Laurens family."

There was so much venom in her last remark that Pierre decided to explain. "Nanette, a family friend, has been visiting in Cologne. She is accompanying us to Strasbourg to attend your father's funeral and to pay her respects to your bereaved grandfather."

Nanette looked at Pierre with irritation. I could see that the cross-languages were going to drive her to distraction. I'm generally not that unkind. I believe that in my wounded state—both mental and physical—I was rising to a challenge and ready to enjoy a much needed diversion. I knew I couldn't compete with Nanette for Pierre's attention, but I would give myself every advantage, as any young girl would.

Orchestra members, who were to play for the dancing that night, were tuning their instruments to play for the cocktail hour. I looked down at my old skirt and sweater, and got up.

"If you'll pardon me, I'm going to change . . ." Then I remembered the seating arrangement in the dining room. "I shall have dinner in my room."

Pierre took my hand. "I won't even consider that. You've been alone all day. I've switched to a larger table. So scamper, and wear your prettiest." His expression hinted at some secret between us.

Unable to understand, Nanette's thin lips compressed into total displeasure.

For dinner I chose another of mother's creations which I hoped wouldn't fall apart. It was of fine, but still firm chiffon, with a fitted bodice. The back was low and fell in soft folds to the waist, and was belted by a black satin cumberbund fastened with a rhinestone clasp. With it I wore mother's single strand of pearls and small pearl earrings.

I shouldn't have bothered. Nanette caught every eye in the dining room when she appeared in a full length gown of some gold cloth that matched her lovely hair. She had applied green shadow that made her eyes gorgeous, and long emerald earrings. She walked like a queen. Pierre looked at me and winked like a conspirator.

Throughout the dinner I observed that Nanette was as irritatingly scornful as Pierre had been when we first met.

A decision had to be made immediately after dinner, and before the dancing, which I was not going to attend. An announcement had been made asking the passengers wishing to take the coach trip to Heidelberg to sign up at that time. I wanted to go to Heidelberg to try to find Michael. At some stop on the trip, I thought that I might attempt to reach him by telephone, a difficult thing for an American in Europe.

In the end, I decided to remain aboard ship. I would write to Michael at the School of Medicine and ask that he write back to assure me he had arrived safely. As I started to my room, I saw Pierre and Nanette dancing. They were such a striking couple that I stood for a few moments watching them. Pierre had called her a family friend, but her possessive attitude told me that she was more than that to him.

I was first to arrive in the main salon the next morning, prepared with my guide book for what father had told me was the most beautiful castle filled area of the river. It was still quite dark as the ship inched toward Rhens and the famous medieval castle perched high on the mountain. The river was wide here and not as sluggish. Swiftly propelled craft passed with winking lights.

I did not go to the dining salon for breakfast, but stayed in a chair far from the two Pierre had chosen. I had a good view. Passengers with cameras wandered in. Trains along the shore darted like swift, lighted snakes.

Cherry orchards in full bloom crept up and down the hills and flowed through valleys like great puffs of clouds into the gloomy dawn. Rain began slowly to fall. By the time morning consomme and sandwiches were served, the music of the Lorelei was played and passengers with cameras jammed the windows while outside crews attempted hopelessly to clear them. I went to my stateroom to watch from my own window.

I did not go to luncheon. I fell asleep watching vineyards crawling up steep rocky cliffs.

I didn't wake up until Pierre knocked at my door. He

appeared concerned.

"I'm sorry I missed luncheon."

"I'm sorry, too. Let me look at your eye. You really have a black one now."

We talked for a few minutes. He wanted me to join them in his stateroom for a glass of wine before dinner, but I excused myself.

After dionner I went down to the small cabin and sat beside father for what would be the last time, all too soon for me. After speaking to the Captain about holding back until all the passengers had disembarked, I returned to my stateroom.

I dreaded what lay ahead. It would have been far better if I had stayed at home in Taos. My apprehension made the next day endless, and the gloomy weather did not help . . .

CHAPTER 9

We arrived at Gare Fluivale in Strasbourg in early dark. Rain fell in torrents. After the boy took my bags, I stood alone in my stateroom staring out at a long black hearse and a grey undertaker's limousine waiting on the quay. I had put on my cleaned and mended raincoat and boots with shaking hands. What awaited me here? Grief and sorrow, but what else? I dreaded to leave this room; here I had felt security. How would I feel in a house full of strangers?

After the other passengers had disembarked, Pierre came for me.

By the time the limousine followed the hearse through rainswept streets and then rapidly down a highway, I had lost all sense of direction. The two machines turned into a road lined with trees that met overhead forming an arch. It was so quiet I could hear the steady splash of tires on the bricks.

At the end of the road, a gate was opened by a guard in a long black slicker and helmet. We passed through formal gardens into a stone courtyard. The large building was shaped like a U. In the darkness and heavy rain all I could see were tall white pillars surrounding the courtyards. As we reached the end, massive double doors opened letting a flood of golden light outline a tall, thin and very straight figure.

Leaning close to the window, I gasped.

"Yes," said Pierre. "That is your grandfather."

"He is so like father. Surely he hasn't been waiting out here all alone." Without waiting for the driver to open the door, I grabbed the handle to run to him.

Behind me, I heard Nanette's voice. "Surely she knows this is Chateau Laurens."

"She expects a house. She has no idea of the vastness of the estate."

By then I was in grandfather's arms, and crying. It had all been too much. Back home, I had thought I had the courage to get through a long trip in a strange land, but I knew now that I needed comforting. He held me and patted my shoulder as I heard the trundle of wheels as the cart was pushed indoors.

Grandfather led me into a large circular hall and across a black and white tile floor toward a curving staircase that swept from a balcony like a bride's train.

Lining the stairway, one on each step, were at least twenty men and women in dark blue aprons and smocks. Lined at the foot of the stairway was a formidable group of men and women.

Grandfather and I stopped while the casket was lifted and placed upon a wheeled table banked by fragrant peonies ranging from deep pink to magenta. I gasped. In every still life and every French scene, father had painted the peonies.

"Yes," grandfather said, "I never forgot Armand's love for peonies. And now that he has finally come home, they are blooming." He took my hand. "Come, Daphne, and meet your people."

A tall woman, wearing a long black formal gown of austere lines and no ornamentation except a large black pearl ring, stepped toward me.

"Daphne," she said in strongly accented English, "I am your Aunt Celeste, your Uncle Alfred's widow. Pierre, who escorted you and your father home, is my son."

"I was grateful to him for coming."

"And Nanette, back so soon?" Her greeting to Nanette was extremely cold and spoken in crisp French.

She embraced Pierre warmly.

Next, we approached a slim blonde woman whose hair was drawn so tightly into a chignon that it made her pale eyes enormous and like what we called goiter-eyes. She waited until grandfather introduced us.

"And this is your Aunt Michele, my son Jean's widow."

She clasped my hands. Hers were moist and trembling. "Accept my deep regrets. I knew Armand. Welcome to your home." Over my head she shot a look of pure hatred at Nanette who after greeting the others, flounced away with Pierre.

Aunt Celeste, blushing a deep crimson, watched them go.

"And your first-cousin, Theresa, Jean and Michele's only child."

Pierre had predicted correctly. Here was an enemy. I had hoped he was wrong. She was the closest to my age of the family and I had wanted her to like me.

"I am sorry about your father's passing," she spoke in a strained and rather weak voice.

I wanted to put my arms around her and let her know that I was prepared to be a friend, but she was so cold looking I merely thanked her. Her face was pale, with sharp lines that emphasized her long narrow eyes that in the brilliant light from the tremendous crystal chandelier, appeared to be colorless. Not only was she cold looking, her hand which barely touched mine, was as cold as a frozen perch. Her interest in me was over as she gazed after Pierre and Nanette.

The next woman was as tall as grandfather with rich auburn hair piled in an aristocratic bunch of curls that made her look as if she might topple at any moment. Without restraint, she bent down and kissed both my cheeks, and hugged me to her violet-scented bosom and exclaimed loudly in a clipped British accent. "Poor child. What a sad journey." Then she whispered, "They haven't even considered that you might want to cry, or go to the dressing room."

My mind instantly called upon the childhood game I used to play with Indian children from the pueblo. We would run into the fields of Indian Paint Brush, tug the petals singing, "Enemy, friend, enemy, friend, where will I end?" Here was a friend. It was as if I had known and loved her always.

Grandfather took her hand and held it. "This is my youngest sister. I thank God for sending her home at this time of my sorrow. Daphne, Lady Olivia Landsdown from London. Your Aunt Olivia. I didn't mention her in my letter. She was on a cruise. My cable caught up with her. She flew from Cape Town in frightful weather to get here."

"I was so thrilled to know that Armand and his lovely Elsa had some happiness and a child. And what a lovely child, so like Elsa. Claude, *where* are the Weills? I most certainly expected Frederich and Louis to come even if Elsa felt that she could not make the trip." Without waiting for my grandfather's reply, she went on to me, "Your cousin was named for your mother. I see facial and coloring resemblance in you cousins. She's a sweet girl. While I am here we shall go across the river to visit her."

"Louis and Frederich are at school in Paris. Elsa sent her regrets. If she'd known you were coming, she would have, I am sure."

"Daphne, this is my cousin, Caren Laurens. He knows more about our business than I do. He handles the selling and distribution of our wines."

I looked up into the coldest eyes I'd ever seen, the exact bluish-green color of icebergs. His long thin face was coldly formal and his thin mouth twisted into what looked like a grimace of distaste as he spoke.

"It is regretful that your visit is a sad one." He didn't regret it for one minute and I knew it even though he stooped to kiss me lightly on each cheek.

At the foor of the stairs, but not on them stood a man so quiet that I hadn't known he was there. Of medium height, with broad shoulders, he was remarkably attractive in formal attire. His hair was dark and neatly cut. His black rimmed colored glasses added a debonair quality to a man whose friendly smile had me liking him already.

He extended his hand. "I am your cousin Caron's assistant, Robert Depris. At your grandfather's request, it will be my pleasant duty to help you learn French."

On the first step stood a heavy set, grey haired woman whose face was creased with smile wrinkles and wet with tears. Catching me in her arms, she kissed me.

"Poor baby. To lose your father and to come so far alone."

Grandfather put his arm around her shoulder. "Aimee took care of your father through childhood and adored him. He was her pet. She will love you."

On and on up the circular stairway. I met stalwart Vallant, grandfather's man, Aubert, the doorkeeper, Alphonse, the head butler, the chef, the pastry chef, the gardeners, kitchen girls and upstairs and downstairs girls; all turned smartly to return to duties or quarters. Many were old with tear-filled eyes. None of them spoke English.

I had been noticing a young girl at the top of the stairs. She seemed to want to dance; she could hardly stand still. She was little and dark with snappy black eyes that smiled brightly at me.

"Welcome, Mademoiselle Daphne. Because of your coming, I am learning to speak English. Is good, eh?"

"You do very well, Linette," grandfather told her. "Linette will be looking after you, Daphne." He embraced me. "Your Aunt Celeste will acquaint you with the upper floors and show you to your rooms. We will be waiting for you in the library. Ring when you are ready and someone will come for you."

Aunt Celeste walked up the steps like a thoughtful queen, studying me as she came. "I'm sure you are much too full of grief to be interested in your father's old home right now. Tomorrow . . ." As she hesitated, I supposed that the funeral had been planned that soon . . all too soon for me. "Another day I will show you your father's suite which has been kept exactly as he left it." Awaiting his return. Poor father.

"Over the years your grandfather has had the rest of the chateau restored. Your father would not have recognized anything except the kitchen and dining room which were not damaged during the war."

We were passing down a broad corridor. I had noticed that at least six corridors led off the balcony. Creamy white wainscoting trimmed in gold came halfway to meet a delicate silk wallpaper. Gold crockets in leaf design had been placed along the ceiling at intervals in the carved and flowery festoon. All of the doors we passed were white with gold trim and exquisite gold hardware. At the third crystal chandelier, which I noted so that I could find my room when I returned from dinner, she turned into a door Linette held open. I stood staring.

"It is lovely, Daphne. The instant he knew you were coming . . . after your first letter and before your father died, your grandfather had the old children's suite redecorated. He pushed the workmen madly. You'll find your grandfather a dear and sentimental gentleman."

This was the reason Linette couldn't stand still. She was dying to show it to me. Without waiting, Aunt Celeste embraced me and closed the door.

Linette grasped my hand to lead me to the windows where she drew the heavy pale blue draperies and white organdy curtains to show me a balcony overlooking a dimly lighted courtyard. Beyond it, on the right, stood a chapel. Far away, outlined against the dull sky, stood the remains of an old castle. I recognized the outline instantly. I had seen it in my father's paintings many times. I knew what lay beyond it, the Rhine. Even now as I looked, a boat passed. Most river traffic stopped for the night. This one appeared to hurry through the rain to a safe port.

Linette pointed toward the ruins. "Jules and I, we meet."

Jules, I guessed, was her sweetheart. I had probably met him on the stairway, but I didn't remember the name. I was to remember it for all the rest of my life...

"The quarters..." As she pointed far to the left I could make out garage doors, six or seven of them. Lighted rooms above evidently were servants' quarters. At the side stood many small houses, most lighted.

Satisfied that she had shown me the view, Linette drew the curtains and draperies and cut out the dreary sound of rain. She turned to face the large room.

This room, done over for me, was larger than our whole adobe house in Taos. The beautiful and shining parquet floor was almost completely covered with Oriental rugs woven of soft blues and rose. Near a large fireplace that had been painted white and trimmed with gold, waited a blue velvet love seat with pillows of blue and rose. On the table in front of it stood a silver bowl holding a huge bouquet of magenta peonies. A small round dining table with a gold and white chair stood in front of one of the two ceiling high bookcases which had been painted white. All of the old books had been returned to the shelves. I kept thinking, "My father played on this parquet floor. He read those books..."

Against the side wall stood a canopied bed larger than my room at home. Evidently it had been brought from some other suite. The top was of blue velvet, but the side curtains, now caught back with velvet loops, were thankfully white organdy. With my claustrophobia I could in no way sleep surrounded by velvet curtains.

Tables with lamps, tables with beautiful statues, and vases, and objects of china had been placed near the windows. Between the windows, with the chair facing the view, was a small gold and white secretary desk, open to display orchid stationary. I knew that at the first possible moment I would sit there and write to Michael. Above the desk hung a large gilt framed mirror.

The walls, wainscoting and paper similar to the hall, held paintings of ladies whom I decided to study another time to determine if they were long-ago Laurens. I walked slowly to stand in front of an early work of father's, a bowl of magenta peonies.

Still twinkling, and practically dancing, Linette tugged me into the dressing room area. This had probably been an old closet holding books. Now the built-in dressing table extended the full length of one side with a tremendous mirror above. The closets, each at least eight feet long and divided by a hall, had mirrored doors. Sliding one open, Linette stepped back to show me that my luggage had already been placed there. The much traveled bags my father had bought for my first trip with him looked incongruous in such a luxurious setting. As I stooped to remove my small bag from the gilt stand it rested upon, Linette drew me into a bathroom that was mirrored and large enough for the Lido girls. A marble top table held two blue washbowls that matched gold dolphins instead of ordinary faucets like we had at home. Linette turned on the water in the tub, and turned me back toward the big room.

"Your keys, Mademoiselle."

Reaching into my purse which still swung on my arm, I gave her my suitcase keys. She helped me out of my

London Fog and hung it in the closet.

In our absence, brief as it had been, someone had put a glass and a carafe of wine and a small platter of cheese on the table, had lighted a fire which threw warmth into the room. Linette shoved me into the loveseat and tugged off my boots. I let myself sink into the soft velvet.

Certainly I was in no way accustomed to such luxurious elegance, but I didn't find it displeasing. Although weary, I felt at home in this room grandfather had planned for my comfort. I sat watching the fire behind the delicately designed brass screen. Had I known what horror lay ahead, or how many nights I would lie shivering in terror in that bed, I could not have relaxed, sipping the light wine.

By the time I had finished a bath scented with rose geranium salts, Linette had pressed and hung all my clothing. The paintings, still wrapped as father had prepared them for the ocean voyage, had been placed on one of the gilt luggage racks. Except for my cosmetic bag, my other luggage was gone.

Linette had already decided what I should wear. She had chosen the black velvet gown with long sleeves which I had made for a winter ball father and I attended in Santa Fe.

Throughout the days of rain in Paris my New Mexico tan had faded. As I cleaned my face, Linette leaned over to examine my black eye which by now had reached full color. She looked at me quizzically until I explained that I had fallen in the rain one night whereupon she began singing a French nursery tune and we both laughed.

I felt guilty about not letting her know that I spoke French, but some inner warning made me quiet. I would be thankful in the days ahead because that was to be my guard.

Linette deftly brushed my hair up and with a few pins made it into an attractive and bouffant arrangement. When she was satisfied with my appearance, she went to the bed, shoved back the organdy and pulled a petit point bell cord . . .

CHAPTER 10

Aunt Olivia came for me. "You look very much better, but you'd better explain that black eye. Everyone is asking about it."

"I fell in Dusseldorf."

"That was Pierre's answer, but he looked so worried, I think everyone decided not to press him."

We did not go down the front stairway, but turned the other way down the corridor and into a more narrow hall.

She stopped in front of a brass elevator. "This thing is an antiquity, but it is better for me than all those stairs. It goes down to the library. This is part of the old building. I'll show you another time that your grandfather restored the two wings of the original chateau. Your father would have been happy. He always wanted it done."

She slammed the elevator door. With a sound I would hear during many nights, the cage shuddered, and with creaks and groans, moved slowly downward.

"At my suggestion, Celeste agreed that we have this small family dinner in the terrace room. That monstrosity of a dining room which Claude has not renovated is too depressing with all of those old family portraits. When I was a child I was so terrified of it I would run through it."

As the elevator landed with a thump of triumph, I saw Pierre and Nanette standing in front of the fireplace. Pierre was devastatingly handsome in formal wear. Nanette, in gold chiffon that left so much exposed I could understand her hugging the blazing fire, leaned toward him as she saw me. Her eyebrows lifted in surprise, thanks to Linette's work. Grandfather was not in the room.

Through the doorway I saw him sitting in the hall, his head on his hand resting against the table. I went to him. He took my hand.

"I was not here when Armand and Elsa left. My old company was reorganizing. Jean and Alfred were with me. Armand had planned to take Elsa home." Reaching up, he pulled a magenta peony from one of the urns and placed it on the casket. "When I came back, they had fled."

His shoulders shook. He had aged in the short time since I had arrived. It was as if he had shrunken. "Some day I will explain. I knew when your first letter came that Armand had never told you about it."

I put my arms around him. "Whatever happened, he loved you always. He yearned to come home." I longed to tell him how through my growing years I had believed my father's grief was all for my mother. "After your letters came, he was a different person. He was so happy to come home."

"He could have come years earlier if I had been able to find him. His mother told me he had gone to fight on the other side."

Aimee came bustling in and pulled him to his feet. "You haven't changed your suit. Now come. Dinner is served."

Grandfather obeyed her as a child would. She bustled on ahead and there was a stirring in the library as the others rose to follow her.

Silently, we walked in a group through the old dining room which had a high beamed ceiling, a long dark table that could have seated fifty, and more than a dozen of the dreary old portraits Aunt Olivia had mentioned. Heavy, dark, red velvet drapes covered windows from the ceiling to the floor. Nanette would be glad we were not dining there; it was cold and musty.

In bright contrast, the terrace room, in one of the new wings, had been decorated in spring green with trellis traced white wallpaper. Sheer curtains had been drawn above the green and white cushions of the window seats. The long oval table of white and gold had been covered with a white linen cloth. A lot has been said about one's surroundings affecting one's moods. Conversation started before Aimee and Alphonse had us seated. Aunt Celeste thanked Aunt Olivia for her suggestion. Caron agreed cynically that it was more cheerful even if it was further from the kitchens and his breakfast eggs were always cold, at which Alphonse's eyes lowered like shades but not before I had glimpsed dismay.

Theresa started to sit down at what must have been her usual place beside grandfather, but Aimee, with a polite murmur to her, eased me into that chair and the first glimmer of hatred shot at me from those cold eyes. Her mother, Aunt Michele, plunked her into the chair next to where Pierre was standing. Just as Aunt Michele started to sit down in a chair that would have placed her beside Caron, Nanette eased into it. A guarded look passed between Aimee and Alphonse. I noticed a pursed lip smile on Robert's face as he touched my arm in passing, and seated himself at my side.

"You will have to get used to having me beside you, Daphne. Your grandfather wants me to interpret for you."

Grandfather reached over under the cloth to take my hand. "French will come easily to you, dear."

We were seated now. Alphonse was pouring the wine. My eyes followed him around the table. Aunt Olivia sat across from me at grandfather's left. Pierre was next with Theresa between him and her mother, Aunt Michele, with Aunt Celeste in what I assumed to be her accustomed place at the other end of the table. Caron sat between her and Nanette. Robert was between me and Nanette. Pierre, with his old scoffing look, followed my glance around the table. When he noticed the three women sitting together, he started to get up, but changed his mind. He held up his glass.

"To my three favorite women."

All of the women smiled. Caron started to make a remark, but coughed instead. Grandfather looked up.

"I intended inviting Father Andre. Aimee, have one of the men run over to inquire if he has had dinner." He turned to me. "Father Andre Lafitte, the pastor of our chapel, will offer your father's Mass tomorrow."

"Father Andre is making a call tonight." Aimee bustled around grandfather making sure that he was comfortable.

The food was delicious, as I was to learn were all of the meals served here. But as always in France I would expect the meal to end when it was just beginning. I was also to learn that French chefs were scientists as well as cooks. No matter how heavy the meal seemed to be, it never left me feeling full. It was as if one course digested the next.

I was busy digesting the course of the various conversations into which both Aimee and Alphonse interposed their opinions. Caron and Pierre had a heated argument about whether or not the excessive rains would damage the grape crop. Aunt Michele, evidently interested in the vineyards, spoke lengthily about previous years. I realized that Caron had not been here too long since his references were always to the crops in Lorraine. Aunt Michele glowed under Caron's interest. Pierre and Aunt Olivia spoke at length about mutual friends in London where Pierre had spent two years with her while attending school there. This bit of information was spicily tossed across the table to me by Aunt Olivia.

"Pierre came to me as a young man and inspired such interest among the daughters of my friends, that they still invite me to their homes in hopes that he will be coming for a visit." She scolded him. "And you haven't visited me for a long time. Now I shall insist that you bring your cousin."

At this both Theresa and Aunt Michele looked up brightly.

Pierre couldn't resist insulting them. He leaned toward the table and said clearly to me, "Daphne, when do you want to go to London? We've just been invited."

After dinner, the others returned to the library for coffee and liqueurs. Grandfather took me out another door and into a corridor that led to his study.

This room was smaller than the imposing library but

still huge by my standards. Completely paneled with a stainy wood, bookshelves lined three sides, all warmed by the fire blazing in the great fireplace between the windows. A fine large desk was centered in the room facing the fireplace and the windows, which I was to learn looked out upon the portion of ancient castle, an imposing view of the river, the chapel, and the beginnings of his vast vineyards.

We sat together on a brown leather davenport which was worn and comfortable. He poured small glasses of the raspberry Framboise which Michael had ordered in Paris, a far place now which had receded as another life might into vague and frightening shadows.

He sat studying me. "Because I feared, wrongly, I know now, that it might be difficult for me to talk to a strange young lady even though she was my granddaughter, I wrote that long and tedious letter to you in Paris. Your cousin Elsa had written that she could not come but wanted you to have the enclosure in case you needed it there." Whatever the enclosure was pleased him greatly.

The letter I lost. Quickly I explained. So that he wouldn't think that I would be careless with one of his letters, and without realizing how much the loss of the letter upset him, I told him in detail of the incident at American Express. He fingered his glass in so much agitation that he had to place it on the table.

"You say the young man who came to your aid thought the attack was intentional?"

"He was a very serious young man. Certainly it was not intentional. I knew no one in Paris, and no one has any reason for wanting to harm me."

He shook his head gravely. "I should have given more thought to inviting you after Armand died. Therefore I must explain."

"I am so sorry, Grandfather. This has all upset you greatly." I wished I had not told him.

Moving closer to me, he told me that in France, upon the death of the head of a family, the estate was divided equally among all the heirs. Knowing that Armand was not only alive but had a child meant to the other heirs that their portions would be somewhat smaller than they had expected to inherit.

"Sadly, it is not all love that has kept what remains of my family together. There is much dissension. Some of us want to keep the vineyards and maintain the estate as one unit. Certainly that has always been my wish. For one thing, with all of my sons gone, it wasn't possible for me to attend to the vineyards and the business. I've never had a good head for business as your father might have told you." This brought a twinkle to his eyes. He was watching the clock on the mantle, I noticed.

"When your father left in the war years, the estate was in a rundown condition and with the departure of most able men from the soil, and the devastation wrought by the bombings, it took years of hard work to build it up to what it has become. Gradually, as men returned, I began marketing the wines, many that had been buried for protection out in the old dungeons." His eyebrows rose in a definite display of pride. "Your father suggested to me that I hide the good vintage there. It was with the money I made from selling the saved bottles that I was able to start rebuilding the damaged parts of the chateau, restore the vineyards, and later the gardens and the grounds . . . which you shall see after . . . the rains stop." He glanced again at the clock.

"Now that I see your youth and innocence, I feel that I must review what I wrote in my letter."

Outside the wind had risen and a shower of rain hit the windows. A draft swept across the floor that was so cold I tucked my feet under the warm velvet of my skirt.

Grandfather shook his head. "There's a loose pane in one of my windows. I've intended asking that it be fixed, but with so much . . ." He got up and poked at the fire.

"I shall have to hurry. At midnight . . . Well, you shall go with me. It was something your father always did with me in the old days. Now to go on. Certain members of the family want to beak up the estate after my death, to sell parts of it, get their portions of their inheritances in cash for travel or other ventures. But it did not occur to me that any one of our family would wish to keep you away, or to harm you for your portion and your father's inheritance. I still can't believe . . . Yet Pierre came straight to me at his first opportunity to tell me of a second supposed attempt on your life . . ." He pointed to my black eye.

I took his trembling hands. "Grandfather, I can't believe it either. Those two incidents were accidents. The doctor on board the ship explained to me that persons grieving are often accident-prone. We can stop any feelings of that kind here. After my father is buried I shall return to my shop and our home. I have no need for any part of their inheritances. Had my father stayed on here, and had I been born here, then I should feel that I deserved to inherit."

"No. No. Surely you would not go home, not at least until I am able to go with you to help you ship your things, especially Armand's paintings, here where I hoped you would make your home. And please don't sell any more of his work."

I stared at him. I had already become so fond of him that I could hardly bear the thought of leaving him.

"We'll get back to that decision later, after you have time to recuperate from your trip and your grief. Pierre told me you got that black eye on a quest for a Black Forest cuckoo clock. Come with me. It is almost midnight. I want you to meet Antoine, my oldest and dearest friend, who is deeply grieved over your father's death."

As I got up facing the curtained windows, the wind slammed one shut. There came a draft of cold air, as it blew open again.

"The window has blown open," I called after him. I ran to fasten it, my hands shaking. I knew instinctively that someone had been standing on the small balcony that I saw when I shoved aside the drapery and fastened the window. How much of our conversation had been overheard and by whom?

CHAPTER 11

Grandfather was waiting for me in front of double doors of thick glass with brass rims. He was looking inside and frowning. When I reached him, he opened the doors.

"Antoine must have stepped out. It isn't like him to leave without locking the doors."

His words were barely audible above the ticking of hundreds of clocks on shelves, tables, and the walls of the L-shaped room. They ranged from great-grandfather clocks lined along one wall to a collection of hundreds of small gold and porcelain clocks in glass cases.

He went to a table holding a clock under a glass hood. He was smiling as he lifted the hood, picked up a key.

"This was your father's greatest joy. He looked forward all year to the winding of the four-hundred-day clocks. He and Antoine packed all of these and had them hidden in the dungeon with the wine."

His eyes sparkled as the hands of the clocks crept toward midnight. "Antoine had better get back. There are six of these to be wound . . ." At that moment all of the clocks began to strike with a glorious cacophony of sounds, bells rang: little bells, big bells, bongs: music played, small clocks tinkled merrily: dozens of varieties of cuckoo clocks fairly shook the walls.

I stood completely enchanted until the din quieted. "I didn't know there were so many clocks in the world, so many different kinds."

"The Laurens have collected them for generations." He began winding the four-hundred day clocks, explaining to me that it must be done with great care so as not to upset the balance of the intricate weights spinning on a slim metal thread.

"Antoine works six days a week, winding and washing the clocks. There are more than seven hundred in the collection. The actual keeping of the clocks consumes eleven hours and forty minutes a day. One day a week I take over because I love doing it. This is my day, but I asked him to take over while I went to my lawyer. I can't imagine where he is. This is one of the most exciting days of his year . . ."

In spite of his worry about Antoine's absence, he continued to wind the four-hundred-day clocks, carefully removing their covers and explaining the age and source of each. They were not old by the standards of many in the collection, but dated to the turn of the century.

When he had finished, I walked over the thick carpeting to the wall of the Black Forest clocks. Many had not been tended; pine cone weights lay on the floor. I started pulling them up and grandfather came to help.

"Antoine has been training a young boy, Bertin Villiers, to take over his work eventually. You must meet him since you will inherit the collection directly from me. It is my own and no longer part of the estate."

I was looking at him in astonishment when a small

late-striking porcelain drew his attention.

"That's some of Bertin's work. He teases Antoine who wants to keep every clock on time." He moved into the L of the room and started behind a large table holding jade clocks. When he stumbled, I ran to him.

We stood looking down upon a crumpled form. The blue smock was stained with blood. A long jeweled knife handle glinted in the light.

Grandfather fell to his knees and caught up the man's body. "Antoine, my very dear friend, you died for me. Daphne, that knife was meant for me. I always wear one of the blue coats. It was my day. I didn't want the family to know that I was going into Strasbourg. I made a point at breakfast that I would be relieving Antoine as usual and if anyone wanted me they would have to wait."

Crying freely, he got to his feet. "No one of them ever comes into this room. It drives Michele crazy. We must call the police." He dropped down onto a red velvet divan. "There is nothing we can do for Antoine. We shall have to take extreme measures of caution. I should never have urged you to come here. I felt the undercurrent of resentment as soon as your first letter came. But it was so intangible that I assured myself I was imagining it. Can you understand that?"

"Yes, I get those feelings, warnings."

"Until we know which one of our household has taken this despicable step, you must stay close to me and your Aunt Olivia. I shall have Aimee make arrangements for Linette to sleep in your quarters." He pondered his plans. "Your Aunt Olivia is the only one of the family who doesn't care about the estate. Her home is in England now and she is quite well off."

Before pulling the bell cord, he stood looking down at Antoine to finally remove his coat and place it over the still form. I could see that the back of Antoine's head did resemble grandfather. Both had fluffy fine white hair worn low upon the neck. From the back, he could easily have been taken for grandfather.

"We are the same age. He worked as a boy in our gardens. He used to spend much time working under these windows so he could hear the clocks. My father invited him in to look at them. He was so entranced that father appointed him 'Keeper of the Clocks.' Antoine studied everything he could find on clocks. After father took him to Furtwangen in the Black Forest to see the magnificent collection there, Antoine began working on repairing them. This is another art he has been teaching Bertin. I shall miss him, as Bertin will. We have been close friends all of my life . . ." He stopped as padding footsteps ran down the hall. "Ah, Aubert, merci."

"Oui, Monsieur?"

My grandfather led Aubert around the table in the L. The knife and blood were concealed by his coat. "There has been a frightful accident, Aubert. Please call the police."

Aubert's friendly face blanched. "Shall I rouse the household, sir?"

Grandfather shook his head. "No. Wait until the police arrive."

Aubert glanced at the windows. "If you are calling in the police, sir, I assume you suspect a break-in. Antoine was so careful in locking the windows."

"The entry must have been made by the door, therefore, it would have been someone Antoine knew."

"Yes, the doors were always locked when he worked." Aubert took grandfather's hands. "This was your day, sir. We took every caution that no one would know I drove you into Strasbourg. If you will pardon me, sir, I would beg you to have Vallant stay in your quarters."

"You're right, Aubert."

As he left, grandfather moved to one of the windows. "We could open a window, hide one of the clocks and let the police consider it a burglary, but I am not good at deceit, and in the end the police would know it was a prideful attempt to hide something, to protect my family." He was so heartbroken and distraught that I threw my arms around him. "And who will help Bertin?"

"I could try, Grandfather. Father had clocks all over our home. And I'm used to handling glass articles in my shop." I didn't add that it would be a way for me to evade some of the unpleasant members of the household until that time when I could go home.

"And I'm very good at climbing ladders. My shop is so small that I keep most things on high shelves."

"Then you must be good at keeping books. Excellent. We must check the catalogs in due time. When you work in here, you must keep Bertin with you . . ."

"Grandfather, isn't it still possible that an outsider did come in here?" I told him about his window being open and that I was positive someone had been listening to our conversation.

He listened with the first hopeful gleam in his eyes . . .

The police came to that conclusion when they lifted Antoine to the stretcher and found an extremely valuable small clock in his hands. The case was antique gold set with mine-cut precious stones.

Grandfather took it into his hands and automatically started winding it for it had stopped.

"No. No," cried one of the policemen. "That must go along with the knife."

"The knife is my own, from my desk in my study. I recognized it."

A hastily dressed Pierre hurried into the clock room. He glanced wildly around at the police who were now taking fingerprints and being cautioned about care in the room by Aubert.

"Has there been a robbery?"

Grandfather introduced him to Commissioner Etienne who told him of Antoine's murder.

"Antoine murdered? He didn't have an enemy in the world. It must have been an attempted robbery. Antoine would have given his life to protect the collection."

"Evidently he did," the Commissioner said dryly.

Pierre gave me a dismayed glance and went to grandfather. "I'm so terribly sorry. He was like a brother to you."

Aimee bustled in, still fully dressed. "Monsieur Claude. You should be in bed. With the funeral tomorrow . . ." She looked shrewdly at all the police in the room and chose the Commissioner. "This is a house of mourning, sir. Monsieur Laurens' last son will be buried tomorrow. If there has been a burglary, and you must inspect the room, these doors can be locked until a later time . . ." She stood with her hands on her hips as she caught a gesture of warning from grandfather.

"The clock-keeper has been found murdered," the Commissioner told her in his toneless voice.

"Antoine? Not Antoine?" Her face convulsed and she was caught as she fell by Pierre and the Commissioner.

Aubert shoved aside a screen and hurried back with a glass of water while the men eased her into the divan just as Aunt Olivia burst into the room and exclaimed loudly.

"What is going on? The little maid in my suite told me she saw an ambulance. Oh, Claude, I was so frightened. I'm so glad you're all right. Who was taken ill?"

Antoine had been a favorite of hers too. She was stricken, and sat down beside the reviving Aimee.

Alphonse appeared in the doorway. He had heard Pierre tell Aunt Olivia and hurried to give his sympathy to grandfather.

It was Alphonse who suggested that the gathering move to a larger and less cluttered room.

The Commissioner ordered two men to stay and continue their work there. "Monsieur Laurens, if you will take me to the desk where the instrument we discussed was kept, we will . . ."

"Yes, Commissioner, and my granddaughter will come with us. She has observed that one of my windows might have been an entry to the chateau."

So it was that I was fingerprinted because I had touched the frame and the lock on the window. The desk and doorframe were fingerprinted also.

Realizing that the members of household were exhausted, and observing grandfather's agitation and grief, the Commissioner took his men and left after telling Pierre they would have to come back to make a thorough investigation which had to include interviewing everyone in the chateau and servants' quarters.

Aubert had sent Vallant to see if Father Andre had returned. He came back with the word that Father Andre's housekeeper did not expect him until morning.

Since I was not to sleep in my own quarters that night, Aunt Olivia went with me to get my night robe and cosmetic bag. She wanted me to take her bed, but I preferred the chaise lounge.

To the dreary sound of rain still falling, I tossed fretfully. The glass pane had not been found. Grandfather suggested to the Commissioner that a workman had taken it since he had asked that it be repaired.

My mind kept repeating over and over the picture of Antoine crumpled on the clock room floor. In the effort to find sleep, I summoned back the cheerful garden room where we had dinner. I regretted Aimee's efforts to please by placing me next to grandfather at the cost of Theresa and Aunt Michele's resentment.

Like grandfather, I couldn't believe that any one of the family could or would go to extreme efforts to harm me, to prevent my coming to Chateau Laurens. Nor could I find it in my heart to accept that one of them had tried to kill grandfather for whom he had mistaken Antoine . . . I hoped that the small pane of glass would be found in the shrubbery, with strange fingerprints. Accepting that an outsider had come to steal, once again I tried to lure the relief of sleep.

But it would not come. I began my old game of enemy, friend, by starting around the dining table where I had got my first impression of my relatives.

That observation assured me of undercurrents of conflict in the family. Aunt Celeste had ignored Nanette at the table. Many times I caught her looking speculatively at Caron during the conversation about the vineyards; she had become especially alert when the interchange was between Caron and Aunt Michele. Often her eyes had shone with admiration for Caron when he got through and made a point. More than once, she had frowned if Nanette spoke to him in a whisper which seemed somehow to suggest an intimacy she denied and which I had thought was an act to irritate Pierre.

I had noticed Pierre's amusement when Nanette flirted with Robert who good naturedly accepted the compliment. Aunt Michele resented Nanette either for personal dislike or even jealousy because Nanette was exceptionally attractive. Or it could be that she wished to encourage the association of Pierre and her daughter.

One thing had come through to me clearly, both Aunt Michele and Aunt Celeste took great interest in Caron. I could imagine what either of the older women saw in him. He wasn't physically unattractive if one didn't let his coldness affect one. When speaking with animation, his eyes, so cold in their appraisal of me, had been handsome with their unusual color enchanced as it was with greying heavy brows. His perfect features could have been chiseled from marble, certainly the thin almost white lips. I could see that some women would call him striking in his overall appearance, that lithe slim body that walked with stalking purpose. About all I noticed in Caron's behavior at the table was his dislike of the easy comradeship so evident between Pierre and grandfather.

Except for a few bitter glances my way, Theresa had been interested only in Pierre. Robert had made a few efforts to draw her into conversation, always difficult across a table, and especially so with heated arguments taking place.

Aunt Olivia was simply charming Aunt Olivia who loved grandfather deeply and seemed to be able to accept the others for what they were and ignore them.

Finally exhaustion took over and I slept until a light knock awakened me. Aunt Olivia, in a dusty pink negligee, ran to answer. A white-faced young maid carried in her tray.

I excused myself to go to my own rooms.

CHAPTER 12

Linette had laid out my black suit and my long black cape. At the sight of the cape, a shiver passed through me. I couldn't imagine why until I remembered folding it in Paris that evening before leaving for the American Express office.

Linette held up the hood and pointed to my light tan London Fog. Since it was still raining I agreed with her that the cape was more suitable for today.

She had drawn the curtains open and placed my tray on a table near the window. I saw that she had been crying. I presumed it was Antoine's murder.

"I'm sorry about Antoine, Linette."

She clipped the top of my egg shell neatly with a small knife before she looked up.

"I do not cry for myself. I loved the old man. I cry for my Jules who is Antoine's great nephew. They quarreled. Jules is heartbroken that they had not made up. He couldn't find him all day yesterday. It was Antoine's day off. Jules believed he had gone into Strasbourg. He did not know until this morning when the police came to ask him about a window pane he was to have repaired. They told him . . . He came to me, crying." She glanced out the window and pointed.

"But you have more to cry about today . . ."

Turning, I saw the cemetery beside the chapel. Workman were raising a long green canopy that stretched from the chapel door.

Grandfather came in at that moment. "I see that you didn't sleep well either, Daphne."

He explained the arrangements that he had made for the funeral, ending with, "Father Andre wishes a moment with you. He will wait downstairs."

Father Andre, a cheerful little round man, pattered back and forth on the black and white tiles questioning me about father's life in America. He was particularly interested in his paintings which I told him about as I ran along beside him. My father's casket had already been removed to the chapel.

Although the distance was short, because of the rain the family, divided in three groups, rode in cars. Under large black umbrellas, the servants crossed the grounds and courtyard. Friends from Strasbourg and the surrounding countryside arrived.

Father Andre carried us through the service solemnly but proceeded toward the cemetery with his brisk little steps shimmying his robes and umbrella . . .

After the graveside service we gathered in a great parlor where I met grandfather's friends and guests. We were served what seemed an endless meal in the dining hall Aunt Olivia found so distressing.

Afterward Aunt Celeste and Aunt Michele took the ladies upstairs. The men gathered in the library.

Aimee bustled up to me. "Come, cherie. You've had enough sadness for today."

She hurried me along to the clock room. After one

horrified glance at my black eye, Jeannine Villiers, who had come with Bertin to offer her condolences, boxed the boy's ears, shoved up his smock to remove a slingshot from his back pocket.

Bertin, an urchin of a boy with a wild shock of black hair and mischievous black eyes, denied vehemently the act as Aimee assured her Bertin had nothing to do with my eye.

Apologizing, Jeannine embraced him proudly. "He is going to find Antoine's murderer. He is furious. But he is a fine boy. His hobby is to sling rocks into the river to raise the water level. I must go. Behave, Bertin."

She had been a governess, Aimee told me, and now taught in the local school.

Bertin couldn't wait for Aimee to leave. With great showmanship and charades, he pushed aside the screen revealing a marble washbasin from under which he drew bottles and jars containing polishes and ammonia. Pouring this into warm water, he dipped a cloth and squeezed it and handed it to me. Seeing that he intended putting me to work, I took off my jacket and laid it on the divan.

With utmost care, and with the finest formed hands I had ever seen, he carried one of the marble clocks to the sink. In pantomine, he showed me how to clean it. After he was sure I understood, he went quietly about his business of winding clocks. I felt right at home. This was something to keep my mind occupied.

I saw immediately that he was capable of doing all of the work himself, and in less time than I could have, and probably less than Antoine.

At the end of our work period, and after I had folded

a stack of damp cloths on the sink because I didn't know what else to do with them, Bertin scooped them into a plastic bag. Standing in front of me, he held up his hand.

"Je sors de la chambre, Mademoiselle Daphne, bonsoir. Et merci." With a delightful bow that swept his rowdy black hair to the floor, he turned and left, his shoulders in the small blue smock held very straight revealing a second and larger sling shot in his other back pocket.

Little did I know that Bertin and his slingshot would save my life in the near future.

I was wandering around the room looking at the clocks when Aunt Olivia came for me carrying a large brass key.

"Come, child. You must dress for dinner. Your grandfather excused himself as soon as the last guest left. He doesn't feel up to coming in for dinner, and will have something sent to his room."

Pierre and Nanette had disappeared shortly after the services. This left cold and austere Caron, to preside over a light meal in the garden room with a preponderance of women. He took grandfather's chair with such an air of authority that I got the feeling he enjoyed it. He continued to pick at Alphonse about his choice of wine, the fish being cold which it was not, the sauce unflavorful, and it was delicious.

Robert and Aunt Olivia managed to keep a light conversation going until we finally filed out through the big dining room into the library for coffee and brandy.

We were just seated when Aubert announced Police Commissioner Etienne. Caron stalked to the door to meet him.

"You've come about the death of Antoine. A dreadful thing."

Theresa reacted as if she'd been stung by a bee. "Why should the police have anything to do with Antoine dying?" she asked nervously.

No one answered her. Caron presented the Commissioner to the ladies and to Robert. I had met him last night.

"I'm sorry. I assumed that you all knew that Antoine was murdered." He drew a large envelope from his pocket and held out the knife. The jewels on the handle glittered in the light.

Aunt Michele gasped. Her protruding eyes fastened on the knife and she grasped Theresa's arm. "It was too horrible, Theresa. I didn't want you to know."

Always pale, Theresa turned as white as cold marble. "But who would want to murder such a harmless old man?"

"That is what we must find out, Mademoiselle, as unpleasant a task as it will be." Theresa stared at him.

"Do any of you know how long it was missing from Monsieur Claude Laurens' desk?"

Aunt Celeste answered. "It has been on the desk from the day I arrived at Chateau Laurens as a bride. Yet I doubt if I would have missed it. I was in Claude's study yesterday morning. It could have been there and it could not have been."

"It could have been taken last night. We've found evidence of forced entry through a study window where a pane was removed. There were muddy footprints on the carpet inside one of the windows. We believe that someone intent upon stealing one or more of the clocks crossed through the study, picked up the knife for a weapon, and proceeded to the clock room. In a large edifice like this that person had to know where he was going." He glanced around. "Where is Monsieur Claude Laurens?"

"He has retired for the night," Aunt Celeste said coldly. "He should not be disturbed after this difficult day."

"I'll see him tomorrow." He drew out a small leather bound book and flipped it open. "Let me begin with you, Monsieur Caron Laurens. Antoine had been dead five hours when discovered. It is my unpleasant duty to inquire where each of you were between six and seven o'clock last evening."

"I can answer for all of us. After the arrival of cousin Daphne, with Pierre Lilliard and a family friend Mademoiselle Nanette Breton who had accompanied Daphne on the last part of her trip, we greeted them and retired to the library for drinks until time for dinner." He looked around the room with raised eyebrows. "Isn't that so?"

Everyone agreed. I sat trying to remember if Antoine had been on the staircase when I came in. I was sure that he had not been.

"If you will pardon me, Monsieur Laurens, I prefer to ask each of you, just for the records, you understand?" He waited politely until Caron nodded coldly. "We must be more specific as to the exact time."

Caron frowned. "I returned home early from my offices in Strasbourg to be on hand for the arrival. I felt that Claude would appreciate my doing so since it was his day to relieve Antoine in the clock room."

The Commissioner's expression did not change, but there was a stillness about him. "I don't understand . . ."

"The clock collection is old and extremely valuable. It is a custom of the family to keep them all in running order and on correct time. Antoine has been clock keeper all of his life. He works a twelve hour day in that room and is relieved one day a week by Claude."

"No one else works in there?"

Caron's eyebrows drew up his forehead in that frosty manner. "Few can stand to even walk in there. Can you imagine working in the midst of seven hundred ticking clocks? It would drive me mad. But yes, a small apprentice, Bertin Villiers, works there. They kept up a constant battle that Bertin worked too fast. Of course Antoine was old and getting fussy."

"Then how was it that Antoine was there on the day that Monsieur Claude usually took over the clocks?"

Aunt Olivia answered for Caron. "Caron was not here earlier in the day when I arrived unexpectedly from Cape Town. My brother was ill with emotion, and stayed in his suite. Antoine agreed to take off another day. My brother thought that Antoine might trust Bertin to do it all alone, but Antoine did not agree to that."

"Thank you, Lady Olivia." He glanced up at Theresa who appeared much agitated. "Mademoiselle Theresa?"

The long narrow eyes squinted. "As you know, it was raining all day. I remained in my room reading. Luncheon was served to me there. I came down at four for tea." She glanced around. "Weren't all of us in for tea from four to five?"

"That's too early. Tell me about six o'clock, please."

"It was six o'clock when Aimee came to hurry me downstairs. Grandfather wanted us all in the main hall when . . . when they arrived from the ship."

"Ah, then you were all in the main hall at six o'clock?"

"Grandfather wasn't. Mother went to his study to look for him. If you are looking for someone who hated Antoine, look to the little creature, Bertin. I have overheard them argue many times."

Caron's thin lips stretched into something between a smirk and a smile. "If Bertin went after Antoine, whom he adored, although they did argue, he would have been far more likely to send one of his exceedingly well aimed sharp pebbles from his slingshot. And he wouldn't have attempted that in his beloved clock room. He would have been more apt to catch Antoine out on the grounds. I have encountered a few of those pebbles. They hurt and leave a bruise and would not be dangerous unless aimed at one's face. Remember, Bertin is a boy small for his age. It isn't likely he would attack a large man and be able to stab him in an area which would be instantly fatal."

I listened to Caron, liking him for the first time.

The Commissioner turned to Aunt Michele whose eyes stuck out like marbles thrown on a pudding. "Oh, dear. I must have passed the murderer. When Claude wasn't in his study, I assumed he was still in the clock room. The door was not locked. I opened it to peer in. The lights were on, but no one was there. All of the clocks started striking six putting up such a devastating clamor that I closed the door immediately."

"Didn't you think it unusual that the door was unlocked and no one there?"

She studied for a moment. "I don't believe I was aware enough. This is a troubled time here. Relatives that one assumed long dead or nonexistent." On that word Aunt Olivia clicked her teeth. Aunt Michele continued without noticing, "Turning up out of nowhere and then one of them dying."

The Commissioner had once again become very still. He was listening intently.

"Was there a window open in Monsieur Laurens' study?"

"Yes. I shoved back the drapery and closed it. Rain was coming in."

"You passed no one in the hall?"

She shook her head. By this time her eyes were like grapes. Her hand flew to her mouth.

The Commissioner nodded. "If your timing is correct, and it was with the clocks striking six, you were in a room with a murderer or a murdered man."

Robert, who had been quietly listening, picked up the brandy bottle, poured a glass and carried it to her. She had turned quite pale.

The Commissioner relented somewhat. "We can be more certain of the time of death later. It could have been closer to seven o'clock. In which case we will have to go through all of this again."

"Now, Madam Laurens." He looked up at Aunt Celeste.

"Aimee and I were rounding up all of the family and the servants. It is my guess that Antoine and Father Andre were the only ones not waiting in the main hall. We were there until six-thirty at which time most of us who were dressed for dinner retired to the library."

"And did you all stay there?"

"Aunt Olivia was going in and out," Theresa volunteered.

"We were all restless and moving about," Robert

said when the Commissioner looked his way. "We had been standing rather a long time."

When he had finished questioning the rest of us, the Commissioner got up to leave. "Does anyone know if any of the clocks are missing?"

Caron shook his head. "Only Claude or possibly Bertin could tell you that. Many of the most valuable are small enough for someone to scoop up a handful worth a fortune. They are catalogued however and at another time Claude can check for you."

Caron and Aunt Celeste moved to the door with him. Aubert was waiting to show him out. Grimly, Caron returned and poured a rather large brandy into all of our glasses.

"This is a most unpleasant happening," he said coldly.

CHAPTER 13

Aunt Olivia and I were first to leave the library. As I looked out from the brass bars of the elevator door, the family had drawn close and were already deep in conversation. Aunt Olivia's hand rested lightly on my arm. She didn't speak until we got off the elevator.

"It seems to me that someone who knew everyone would be in the great hall chose that time to go to the clock room, and that he assumed Claude was there and not Antoine. It could have been anyone of the servants or the family since there was much moving about until just before you arrived."

"Grandfather was at the door . . ." How like my father he had looked standing outlined by the lights.

"Yes, he had been out there for a long time. When he saw the cars coming, he pushed open the doors. I scolded him for standing so long in dampness."

We had reached my door which stood open. Aimee and a red-eyed Linette were arranging a tall folded gold patterned screen to surround a chaise lounge which had been placed near the windows. Linette's petit point bag waited beside the desk. She nodded when she saw us.

Aimee's pleasant face showed the strain of what must have been a difficult day for her.

"Cherie, your grandfather insists that Linette sleep in your room."

"I am to protect you, Mademoiselle." Nipping down, she drew a slim knife from her garter.

"I'm sure that won't be necessary, Linette," Aimee told her sternly. "And you might cut yourself."

I woke up to find that Linette had already folded the screen and removed the bedding from the chaise lounge. She came in with my tray. There was a note on it from grandfather. He was ill with a cold and would I come to see him.

When I had dressed, Linette led me through a dismaying number of corridors to his door. Vallant, in his blue smock, answered the knock. I stopped in the middle of the entry room to stare at early pictures painted by father and framed in the ornate gilt frames he had made all of his life. They reminded me that I still had the three paintings he had chosen to bring to grandfather.

Grandfather, his white hair fluffed like a brown dandelion, was propped up by pillows and enjoying a hearty breakfast. He smiled and pointed with a slice of toast to a gilt and satin chair. Before leaving the room, Vallant poured a small cup of fragrant coffee and placed it on the table.

Grandfather leaned back into the pillows. "That's my own concoction, Daphne. I've been drinking it for years. Coffee, chocolate and brandy with a dollop of whipped cream."

"It's delicious."

"I've had a long conversation with Commissioner Etienne. Something that was said last night in the library makes him think, as I do, that it was I who was meant to die rather than Antoine. He prefers to keep his suspicions from the rest of the household. Since he wants an immediate inventory of the clocks and I am not up to taking it at this time, he is sending an antique expert to help Bertin. He shall remain in that capacity in the household until the Commissioner is satisfied."

"Bertin will be furious."

"I'm sure he will be. Although he is very young for the responsibility, he is qualified, but not to take the inventory. Now as for you and your protection, I've asked Robert to start your French lessons this afternoon, not that I think you need them. I observed at dinner and during the reception that you understand it."

I nodded. I hoped that none of the rest of the family had been so observing. It wasn't that I intended to spy on them, but I knew I could learn more about them and protect myself if they were unaware that I understood their conversations.

"Since Robert has been a trusted employee of Caron's, but is not of the family, I told him that I would appreciate his looking after you. When he isn't on hand, spend free time with Monsieur Rochelle in the clock room. Bertin will be expecting to train you." His eyes twinkled. "This morning, Olivia wants you to go with her through the chateau. She hasn't seen all of the alterations and we want you to know your way around."

I was glad he had planned this. The chateau was so large that I doubted I could even find my way from his suite back to my own. The confusing part to me was the balcony off the main hall. I had no idea which corridors led to private rooms and which ones went down the new Ls that enclosed the large and bare courtyard at the front.

"I still can't believe that our lives are in danger."

"Your father may have told you that I have always been a sentimental man and one who is prone to see life in its most exaggerated proportions. While this has been a disadvantage many times over the years it has proven to be almost second sight. Do you follow me, Daphne? You are so young. One gets feelings of danger, of apprehension that it would be foolhardy to ignore. I believe that two attacks on you have already been made, the one in Paris and the night Pierre so carelessly left you alone in Dusseldorf." He looked at me questioningly.

I admitted it. "Yes. I suppose they were, grandfather. I simply was unable to believe it."

"Then we will each of us take precautions. At least until we can discover which of our relatives would want a larger share of the estate. You are in greater danger than I, I believe. After all, I am a very old man. My natural years are numbered. None of this surfaced until I sent for you. No, don't be alarmed. I'm so happy that you wrote. I am grieved that I did not fly to New Mexico while Armand was still alive so that I could have known him again. But I have you in his place and I am grateful."

I hugged him, and removed his tray. There were three doors leading from his bedroom. The first one I tried was the bathroom. The next was a completely modern kitchen.

He was smiling when I came out. "When the remodeling was going on I remembered the years of eating cold meals that had come up the dumb waiter or had been carried the long way from the kitchens. I had small kitchens placed in all of the master suites. Light meals can be prepared. Food from the kitchens can be warmed, dishes washed, wine chilled . . . All very satisfactory."

What a delightful old gentleman he was. I was getting up to leave because I did not want to tire him. He looked so careworn and grieved. Vallant showed Aunt Olivia in. She was like spring in a deep pink knit suit. With a bright wave to grandfather, she took my arm.

"I've just heard that the weather is clearing. Before too long I can take you on a few outings I've planned." She called back over her shoulder. "Get rested, Claude. You must go back to England with us for a visit."

Aunt Olivia wanted to start in the kitchens because Aimee would soon be involved in preparations for the noon meal. I found them and the pantries large enough for a hotel. A modern dishwasher had been installed between four sinks, separating sinks for dish and vegetable washing. A chef wearing a tall white cap was snapping pods of fesh peas and popping them into a colander. Another raised the lid of a steaming pot to show us crab bisque prepared at Aunt Olivia's request. As one of the girls led us to inspect one of the pantries, Aimee bustled in.

"Come, cherie, these are our kitchen gardens. We grow our own vegetables and fruit. Now we have only chickens. In former years we kept our own animals. When Monsieur Caron came from Lorraine he insisted to your grandfather that it was less expensive to buy meat in quantity from his friends and store it in freezers. We do it except for fish we buy." Her disapproval of

Caron's suggestion was evident.

From the kitchen she led us down the paneled hall with glass door cabinets that held the chateau china with the familiar coat of arms. There must have been service for a hundred.

"It was your father who had us pack all of this and the crystals to store down in the ruins with the wines. I hate to think where your grandfather could have started after the war had it not been for the sale of the old vintages. Unfortunately some of the crystal wasn't packed well enough and had to be replaced. Armand's plans also saved all of the silver." She threw open great cupboard doors.

"Before the evacuation poor Antoine finished packing the clock collection and came here to help us pack these things, but in truth he cared for nothing but the clocks. When everything was placed in the dungeons, Armand helped the men pour concrete and stick it full of rocks. He was so artistic, no one could have guessed he was not looking at old ruins. If this had not been done, little would have been saved. Even then, Armand and his bride did not know how soon after they left that the chateau would be evacuated..." Her nice eyes met mine. She had not intended to say anything about my mother.

"Where did you all go during the evacuation?" I asked Aunt Olivia as we hurried through the old dining room she so disliked.

"I urged Claude to come to England, but of course, he went into the war, as did most of the men. The women were last to leave. Many went to villages in Switzerland with friends or relatives. Many simply went to small villages in the Vosges Mountains. They were all so scattered, no one knew whom he would not find when he returned. My husband and I traveled to the Bahamas in his yacht."

"It must have been dreadful."

She shoved open great sliding doors that I had not noticed in the dining room. Beyond waited one of the most delightful sitting rooms, all green and gold and white. Aunt Olivia clapped her hands. Running to the windows, she drew back the shades of heavy green silk brocade. Beyond, lay an expanse of wide lawn extending to flower gardens flowing into a line of new greenhouses.

She pointed out the thickness of the window frame. "This is part of the original chateau. As children Claude and I were sent in here to play with visiting children during bad weather or when lawn parties were in progresss. We could watch through lace curtains, but we couldn't escape. There was no door other than through the busy dining room, and a sheer drop to the lawn prevented our attempting it that way." Moving to a newly finished panel, she slid it open. We stooped to peer into an opening. A dank chill invaded the room, passing over us. She pointed upward. "This is one of the old dumbwaiters. Often we would crawl through here to the kitchens. Down the other way, where the draft came from, is a horrible ladder-stairway that leads to a tunnel. It had been long forgotten. Once, when we were beyond the age of caution, Claude and I took lanterns and went down. We followed a tunnel for a long distance and came out in the dungeons. Your father and his brothers discovered it in their day. It was through that tunnel that the last of the valuables were carried and hidden. Long after the rubble was cleared away, many years after the war, Claude had the cement cover removed to bring up the wine so it wasn't necessary for the tunnel to be used. Can you imagine how frightening it was to children?"

With my claustrophobia I could imagine it only too well. In spite of the beauty of the room, I wanted to be out of it.

The grand ballroom was also in the old building, and had had to be restored. Grandfather had chosen white and gold which enhanced the parquet floors. The orchestra platform in the shape of a giant seashell stood golden against white tapestry walls lined alternately with small round tables, chairs and huge mirrors.

"Probably this will never be used until one of you young people marry. I stand here and dream of the old days when all of Strasbourg entertained in a manner almost forgotten today."

My mind immediately associated Pierre and Nanette, transporting them chimerically to this room from the salon on the ship where I had watched them dance.

"I suppose Pierre and Nanette will be the first . . ." I hoped she didn't notice how wistful that sounded.

"I would rather see Pierre marry Theresa in spite of her total lack of charm. Nanette doesn't appeal to me as a proper wife for Pierre."

"She's very beautiful."

"A classic beauty. She's a model, you know. Michele tells me she shows up here every time she isn't working."

"That must be very pleasing to Pierre."

"He is often surprised."

By this time we had reached the clock room. That

gorgeous little urchin with his broom of black hair bowed to us. "Madam and Mademoiselle. Come in and see how I have taught Monsieur Rochelle to clean the clocks. He has been a great help to me in my work."

"Little rascal," Aunt Olivia said to me in English.

Monsieur Rochelle looked up at us and merely nodded with no trace of amusement on his solid stern face. He was a sturdy man whose strength seemed to burst out from the too small blue jacket he wore. There was about him an air of readiness. He was a man grandfather would be glad to have in the chateau. Even Aunt Olivia did not know that he was a policeman.

"I haven't met you, sir."

He introduced himself in a calm matter of fact voice. "I am a clock expert. Monsieur Laurens has hired me to take a full inventory. Until the books arrive, Bertin is putting me to work."

Aunt Olivia was as opposed to visiting the occupied suites as I was. Since these for the most part were in the new wings, we stayed in the old building.

As we entered my father's room the sun broke through the gloom and filtered a fine dust into a shaft of gold touching his easel where still waited an unfinished sketch of the ruins we could see from his windows. Father had completed that identical scene many times in my lifetime. Seeing his desk, his bed, the boyhood mementos—all seemingly untouched by the war that had rent his life, left me silent and filled with longing. Grief leaves a lonely emptiness, a hollow void that is never filled, never warm, around which unrelenting yearning tugs . . .

CHAPTER 14

At the dining table Robert brought forth a small French grammar.

"May I suggest that you get a wrap. We should take advantage of the sunshine since the rains are predicted to continue this week."

I was wearing a black wool dress and serviceable shoes. Before visiting grandfather I had expected to spend the morning climbing a ladder to wind clocks. I went to my suite and got my black cape.

As we walked, Robert began basic French by naming each bush or tree or bench that we passed. I repeated the words. We were soon into simple sentences.

"You either have a remarkable memory to grasp these words so quickly or you've studied French."

"Yes, in high school."

"I noticed at the table that you seemed to react to parts of the conversation. It occurred to me that perhaps you and your father had conversed in French. It was his native language. Your grandfather assumed that you spoke only English because your letters to him were not in French."

It had not occurred to me when father was so ill to even consider a difference in languages. I couldn't possibly have composed a letter in French. I told Robert so.

We were passing the chapel. I turned to take the path around it to the cemetery. I had been wanting to go to my father's grave.

I stopped to look back at the chateau. I hadn't on the day of the funeral. From this angle, it was a handsome building of native stone that was pink in the sunshine. The original and the new blended well but the lines were clearly visible. The mansard roofs were built of layered dark green tiles interspaced with many tall chimneys. A great nest had been built on what I guessed from the large windows was the ballroom chimney. As I gazed a stork flew to it and dropped down awkwardly.

"How lovely."

"Odd looking birds, aren't they? They're supposed to bring good luck to a household. Let's hope this one does."

With a gay tapping on the paving stones, a pony pulling a small cart swept around the chapel and we got a cheerful greeting from Father Andre. An empty market basket bounced around on the seat beside him. Robert looked after him fondly.

"Charming old love. He's always inviting me to come to services. I think he's trying to convert me."

The cemetery was much larger than I had noticed, and arranged like a park with trees and flowering plants. The family plot, enclosed by an ancient wrought iron fence, covered an extensive area. Someday before leaving France, I wanted to look at the old markers. And I would ask grandfather if we had cousins elsewhere. There were so few Laurens left.

We sat on a wrought iron bench. The damp air wafted to us the fragrance of the peonies now in full glorious bloom. From this point I saw for the first time the old ruins that had been shadowy in the rain. Of the same pink stone as the chateau, worn and ancient broken shafts of pillars and chimneys were climbed over by vines and trees. A few vaulted arches remained, and one long row of small windows. Beyond it, far below, the Rhine stretched with its never-ending traffic of ships and small bateaus.

Robert handed me the grammar and asked me to read from it. Fortunately, he had to correct most of my pronunciations. His colored glasses fascinated me. They had turned darker still in the sunlight, and had small round reading areas at the bottom. His coloring was dark so I presumed his eyes to be brown or black and probably weak. His manner was always pleasant and although he had seemed at ease the few times I had seen him, today I observed a tremor in his hands as if he were nervous.

I attributed this to my father's funeral, the horror of Antoine's murder, and the fact that spending time with me took him from his regular duties.

"This lesson is going to be valuable to me. May I keep the grammar with me? I'll be better prepared for the next lesson. It seems a shame to take you from your work."

"Not at all, Daphne. My work varies. I travel on occasion for Caron, or do special work in his office. Quite often I attend to your grandfather's correspondence. Being adept at languages, it is my good fortune to take care of the many foreign visitors to the vineyards, customers from abroad. I've become a fairly good guide. One day you must let me take you to the wine presses. If you have not seen the workings, you will be astonished at the simple and the complicated methods of wine making."

"Thank you. I'd like very much to do that." I felt that today's lesson was over and I wished that he would leave so that I could go over to father's grave. Also, I was uncomfortable in my heavy cape and flung it over the back of the bench.

We reviewed the lesson. In addition to learning to speak French so that I could be understood, I learned to read in Robert's full dark eyebrows the expressions that one usually finds in another person's eyes. Now he registered annoyance and I looked up to see Pierre and Nanette approaching. Nanette was stunning in an ice green coat and smart beret to match.

She greeted me as absently as she usually did and spoke in her staccato way to Robert, not aware that I understood her words.

"I've always thought you looked much more like an athlete than a secretary or a teacher, and what a shame to waste such a beautiful afternoon."

"In no way a waste, Mademoiselle." He said it so sharply that Pierre, who had been looking at the river, turned and sat down beside me.

Taking my hand, he patted it absently. "One evening soon the four of us should go into Strasbourg. Daphne has not yet seen the city. We should have done that today. More rain is forecast. I am beginning to worry as is Claude."

"And the others have been alarmed," Robert told him.

"Do come on, Pierre. We need the exercise."

Pierre gave my hand a squeeze, and followed her. I got up, hoping to put an end to the lesson. I walked over and broke off a magenta peony and carried it to my father's grave. Robert followed and stood beside me.

"Nanette is right. We need exercise too. Come along."

We took the path on the other side of the chapel back to the courtyard which was larger than a city block at home in Taos. We stood for a moment looking down at the old tree-filled moat of ruins. Stone steps led downward into the jungle.

"Would you like to explore? The view from the wall is wonderful. You can look right across into Germany."

The strange part of this was that as we approached the ruins, I wanted very much to explore them. But when looking down into the moat, a morbid fear rose up almost choking me in the way severe claustrophobia affected me. I wanted to turn and run. I didn't even want to try to interpet this sudden trepidation.

"Not today, thank you. I'd rather go over there to the cherry orchard."

"You'd really enjoy having the experience of seeing where your ancestors guarded their part of the river. There is a base of the old toll gate still in the river. We could stand on that portion of wall . . ."

That was all he needed to say. I would never stand on any portion of the wall to gaze straight down into the river. It made my knees weak to even consider it.

Even though Robert had been intent upon showing me the ruins, I resolutely trudged on to pass what I had come to think of as Linette's and her Jules' trysting place, a seat-like rock worn smooth by centuries of lovers meeting, secluded in a clump of elm trees.

Reluctantly, Robert followed on the stone path leading to the three story pink stone building housing six garages. He told me the two stories about them were servants' quarters. Behind the building were attractive small cottages each with a garden. Beyond them was the cherry orchard that had appeared to be in full bloom from the ruins. As we drew nearer, I saw that the earth beneath was matted with fallen blossoms and only enough to give the pink glow I had seen remained on the wet and shining red limbs.

By now we had made a half circle to come up into the kitchen gardens.

"I shouldn't go wandering around the grounds alone if I were you. Your grandfather has told me that two attempts were made on your life, one in Paris and one in a stop your ship made at Dusseldorf."

Stooping to pull a weed from the asparagus that lined the walk, I wondered at grandfather taking Robert into his confidence.

"I'm still not convinced they weren't accidents."

"If they were attempts on you, one thing sure is that would eliminate anyone here. Do you know if the family were at home at the time?"

"You would know that better than I."

"I was away on a business errand for Pierre."

"You know that Pierre met me at Rotterdam and traveled with me."

The eyebrows rose above the line of the sunglasses. "Did he fly down? No, I suppose he took the train. Weren't you able to give the police a description of the assailant?"

"The police weren't called, and I couldn't have given them a description. Each time the attack was sudden.

131

I'm afraid I am not very observing. But if I ever saw him again, I might . . ." A small kitten immediately followed by a little girl bolted toward us down the path and we leaped aside into the asparagus. When she had caught the kitten, the little girl brought it for my admiration. After a while, she let me hold it, a fluff that was big eyes and long tufts of white fur.

Robert was still worrying about my attacker. "How could anyone have recognized you?"

"It would have been easy in the American Express mail line. I said my name distinctly."

"I believe your grandfather mentioned that you had a friend with you."

"He wasn't with me. He came to my aid after my arm had come in contact with a very sharp knife."

"That's a mild way to put it."

"Well, I'm still not sure."

Robert left me at the door of the clock room. Bertin and Monsieur Rochelle were occupied cleaning clocks. I had noticed a small writing room off the main hall. Since I still wanted to explore the great courtyard beyond it, I went in there to write my note to Michael who had come so swiftly into memory as Robert questioned me about Paris.

This small room overlooked the spacious courtyard. On each side was a long corridor. The pillars I had seen in the rain, when we arrived at the chateau, were actually arches—looking so much like those of our New Mexican architecture that I became desperately homesick. Wrought iron benches were placed under windows at intervals down the corridors. The balustraded balconies running the length of both new Ls formed the roofs of the arcades. Great pots of flowering bushes stood at each arch that ended at the formal gardens. Beyond the gardens stood the gate and the gatekeeper's stone house. I could imagine that old courtyard of flat grey stones during a pageant in the Middle Ages. Certainly there was room for one in that formidable place.

Dropping the curtain, I turned to the apple green desk and removed paper and an envelope of the orchid Chateau Laurens stationery. I wrote to Michael at the School of Medicine at Heidelberg. When I finished it was tea time.

I was startled when Aunt Michele, who favors flat soft-soled shoes, fluttered into the room. Blinded by the sunlight, her prominent eyes searched the room to enlarge at the sight of me, whom she acknowledged with a nod.

"Tea time, Daphne," she said, picking up a book that had slipped down the side of a velvet cushion of a deep and comfortable looking chair. After she left, I stood looking at the chair. Facing the stairway as it did, and the great main hall, it afforded a perfect view. Anyone sitting there could watch the stairs, the main doors, and the two corridors leading to outside doors at the beginning of each L. And, since my tour of the chateau that morning, I saw that anyone sitting here also commanded a view of the corridors extending one on each side of the main hall to outside doors, the one near the clock room which had been used to go to the chapel for father's funeral, and which Robert and I had taken today . . .

There were no stamps in the desk. Mine were upstairs in my room. Since no one had come for tea except Aunt Michele, I hurried upstairs.

Linette, who had been dusting, turned. "Mademoiselle, where is your cape?"

I blinked. I had dropped it back on the bench in the

cemetery and forgotten it. I walked to the window to look down. It was still there, draped over the back. Clouds were moving in swiftly. Linette, who had followed me to the window, put down the dusting cloth.

"It's going to rain. I'll go get it."

Fixing a stamp on the envelope, I took it to grandfather's room, and gave it to Vallant who would see that it was posted. Grandfather was resting. It had already begun to rain.

My windows had been open. I ran back to close them. In the gathering darkness, I saw Linette running in my cape toward the old ruins. Poor little thing, going to meet her grieving Jules . . . I went on down to join the family for tea.

CHAPTER 15

After tea, I joined Monsieur Rochelle in the clock room. Bertin had gone home for dinner. He would return to relieve Monsieur Rochelle to have the evening meal with us at grandfather's suggestion, so that he could observe other members of the family. Father Andre would be there also.

"You understand, Mademoiselle, that only you and your grandfather know that I am a member of the police detective squad?"

"Yes."

"Commissioner Etienne has been quietly interviewing the servants in their quarters. He prefers not to see the family again until a few days of mourning pass. He's talked with your grandfather quite frequently. After one of those conversations the suggestion came that I dine with the family. Madam Celeste wrote a note inviting me."

He questioned me about my encounters in Paris and in Dusseldorf in such detail that I had not realized how late it had become until Bertin raced in with a dripping umbrella which he placed in the sink.

I got up. "Pardon me, Monsieur Rochelle. I must dress for dinner."

"So must I. I'll accompany you to the elevator."

Caron and Pierre, attractive in their formal attire, were already having apertifs and an argument in the library. They stood as we entered, but as the elevator started to rise, resumed their argument. As usual, it was about the rains and vineyards.

Linette had not returned. Hurrying my toilet, I chose the same black velvet gown which was warmer than my others to wawlk through the long cold corridors. As I left, I drew the draperies against the sound of the dreary rain. I was thinking about grandfather's vineyards. Vallant had reassured him that the summer sun would make the grapes plump and sweeter because of the rain.

As at tea time, Antoine's murder was the topic of conversation. Everyone except Aunt Michele, evidently to Theresa's horror, believed that an outsider had come intent upon theft.

Aunt Michele leaned toward Caron. "I'm not too sure, Caron. Two of the upstairs girls were discussing a quarrel Antoine and his nephew Jules had in the courtyard the day before the murder."

"And you stood listening of course," Caron said contemptuously.

Theresa turned ashen. Alphonse jumped to retrieve the fork she dropped and replace it with another. Monsieur Rochelle unobtrusively put down his knife and fork and picked up his wine to sip it with intense interest in the flavor as Father Andre quietly objected to Aunt Michele's words.

"Jules and Antoine were devoted. Of course, they did quarrel, as did Antoine and Bertin. We must remember that Antoine was getting old, and as in some cases, a bit senile which makes one apt to be more quarrelsome. We must trust the police to find the person who broke in that night. When the case is solved Jules must accept that it was death alone that interfered with his intentions to apologize to his uncle. He came to me with his grief. I have spoken to Aimee. Jules is fond of her and she is good with the young people when they are troubled."

As if Father Andre had called Aimee, she appeared in the doorway, soaked and stricken. Glancing wildly around the table, she rushed to Father Andre.

"Oh, come quickly. Monsieur Caron, come too."

Annoyed, Caron stood up and threw his napkin to the table. "Now what, Aimee. It isn't enough that the food is cold and . . ."

Aimee stared at him blindly. "Linette, Jules has found her . . ." As she began to topple, Aunt Olivia placed her in her chair. "That child is dead," Aimee cried. "Jules had looked for her all evening. They were to meet. Since it was raining, he went to her home. He waited. She'd been lying in the moat . . ."

I gripped the arms of my chair. Linette, wearing my cape, had been running near the moat when I last saw her . . .

Caron, almost blue with anger, ordered the astonished Alphonse to bring his rain gear and umbrellas. Monsieur Rochelle slipped out behind Father Andre.

While he waited, Caron took a long draught of his wine. Pierre, who had slipped to the kitchens, returned with lanterns and a long flashlight.

"If we hurry, Caron, we might catch whoever is in the grounds."

Caron's eyebrows rose, then his face cleared. "Why, of course. Aimee, call the gate keeper. Call the police."

It was apparent Aimee was not up to anything. Aunt

Olivia went into the library to make the calls. My first fear now was for grandfather who would see the lights and hear the police coming. I got up . . .

Pierre took my arm. "All of you women go into the library. Stay together. Don't one of you leave. You must realize the danger. There is a murderer among us, someone of the chateau."

"Pierre," Aunt Michele shrieked, her eyes popping. "How dare you?"

"You know I don't mean of the family."

I tried to get Pierre's attention, to finally draw him aside. "Pierre, Linette was wearing my cape. I'd left it in the cemetery. When the rain started, she went down for it. I saw her running toward the moat."

"When?" His face was white and his grip on my wrist like iced steel.

"As I was coming down to tea."

"Late, I believe," Robert, who had come to my side, said quietly.

"Good heavens," exclaimed Pierre. "Don't make remarks that sound so insinuating."

I had not thought Robert's tone insinuating at all. In fact, I didn't remember Robert in the library when I went in. I caught a movement at the table. Theresa had gone to her mother still frozen in her chair. They were speaking softly. Theresa pointed to me and exclaimed.

"She started all of this. We were a peaceful family, a happy family until she appeared." She was crying now, obviously distraught.

Aunt Michele looked frightened; Aunt Celeste, furious. At the sight of her face, Aunt Michele drew her daughter to her.

"The poor child, always sensitive, is frightened, as we all must be, if we have good sense."

Aunt Celeste picked up her wine glass and started into the library.

"Sensitive my eye," she muttered as she passed me.

Pierre had gone with Caron. At my side Robert hesitated. "I merely observed that you had come in late. I certainly didn't mean anything else. If I did, I meant that I was glad it was not you wearing the cape."

So he had overheard me . . .

I went to Aimee who sat so still, staring at the table cloth. Urging her to rise, I led her into the library to a chair close to the fire. As I stepped to the table to pour a sherry for her, Nanette crept close to Theresa as they passed through the doorway and said softly,

"Yes, if I were you, I should aim blame at some other girl, the way I've seen you carrying on with Jules."

Cold and colorless Theresa showed the first real sign of vitality I'd seen yet. Her face flamed.

"I should be quiet if I were in your shoes, Nanette. You are not the only one who creeps around at night spying upon others."

"You know very well what Jules and his uncle quarreled about. Jules is a handsome boy and you have pursued him shamefully."

I stood transfixed with the sherry bottle in my hand. This was the first time my apparent inability to understand French had served me well. Nanette ignored my presence as she usually did. Theresa was too upset to notice if a bomb had fallen into the room. Aunt Michele and Aunt Celeste were busy arguing. Aimee simply stared into the fire. Aunt Olivia turned from the telephone and went to her.

Theresa had turned her back to the room and faced Nanette in fury. "And you are going to tell that? When you do, prepare yourself to face up to Pierre that you . . ."

Unfortunately for me Aunt Michele called out loudly for Theresa who whirled on her heel and went to her mother.

Nanette looked after her thoughtfully, and came to the table Alphonse had already prepared with coffee and cups, the usual liquors and liqueurs and the ice bucket. As she saw me standing there holding the sherry bottle with what must have been total amazement on my face, hers convulsed with laughter.

She poured a stiff scotch over ice and said to me in her fast French, "Little kitten, it is a good thing for me that you don't understand French." Her eyebrows rose thoughtfully over her eyes and with a clear look of victory she added, "And a very good thing for that one over there."

I smiled as if she had made a pleasantry and carried the by now full glass of sherry to Aimee.

Aimee was coming up out of her shock. As she sipped the sherry, her eyes took on the horror she had witnessed. She began crying uncontrollably in Aunt Olivia's arms.

"I knew," she said. "I could have saved Linette. I could have saved Antoine." Looking up, she gazed straight at Theresa with an unfathomable expression and then looked away just as quickly, but not before Theresa had noticed.

I watched a cold look cross those icy eyes before she resumed her talk with her mother about a gown she had seen in Strasbourg. They had already dismissed Linette's death, she was after all just one of the many young girls who worked at the chateau. Her death was a shame, but it did not affect their lives.

And Linette had died for me, just as Antoine had died for grandfather. The murderer would not make three mistakes . . .

I had to get to grandfather. He would see the lights and be frightened. Or he would call Alphonse . . . Perhaps Alphonse had already called him. I got up.

"Aunt Olivia, I'm going to grandfather."

"We had all better obey Pierre. He is wise." Reaching up, she tugged on the petit point cord that usually summoned Alphonse and it was most often Caron doing the ringing to make a complaint. I thought irrelevantly that if Caron were next I would know who killed him.

A tall blonde kitchen girl answered. "Oui, Madam?" She spoke to Aunt Olivia, then looked down at Aimee still in tears. "Madam, Aimee has not had dinner. It would help her. And we are waiting."

It appeared that Alphonse had not told them about Linette. They would know it soon enough. Aimee placed her emptied sherry glass on a table. Her words reflected my thought.

"They must be told. Alphonse merely told them that there had been some trouble." Straightening her shoulders, she went out with the girl.

Aunt Olivia got up. "We'll go together. No one will tackle the two of us. I want to see how Claude is taking this, if he has already been told. I imagine the police were sent on around by the gate keeper." She pressed the bell for the elevator.

The four women in the room turned to look after us as the cage began to lift . . .

A grave Vallant opened the door. "Be seated, Lady Olivia and Mademoiselle Daphne. Monsieur Claude is engaged."

Aunt Olivia nodded briskly. "The police, I suppose."

"Yes, Madam."

Since Aunt Olivia's honest but strident voice carried enough to rouse the whole chateau, grandfather called out.

"Come in here, Olivia."

As Aunt Olivia entered, Monsieur Rochelle came out.

"I was coming to look for you, Mademoiselle." Nodding to Vallant, he guided me on out the door into the main balcony. "Let us go somewhere where we can talk without being overheard."

"Why not the clock room? Everyone expects you to be there."

"Yes, of course. That is good since Commissioner Etienne wishes me to continue in the same capacity in spite of this case being closed."

Closed? The case closed? They had caught the murderer. Holding up my long velvet skirts I padded down the staircase after him. But he did not resume speaking until we had passed the silent library door and gone on to the clock room.

Going to the refrigerator under the sink, he tugged out glasses and a bottle of wine I knew Pierre had chosen for him. Handing me a frosted glassful, he indicated the divan where grandfather had dropped in such dreadful dismay only a few nights ago when we had discovered Antoine's body . . .

"The Commissioner has preferred not to tell your grandfather that the boy Jules who was Antoine's nephew and Linette's fiance believed he had found you. Linette was wearing your cape. She was lying face down on the side of the moat. The gun was at her side. Picking up the gun, he called out for help. Men came from the garage where they had been working on a car. Jules was holding the lantern when they turned the girl over. He started screaming when he saw it was Linette. He was still screaming when we got there. He has been arrested for both murders."

I did not know the boy. If I met him on the stairway upon my arrival, I did not remember. That did not lessen my shock nor my disbelief.

"He loved his uncle. He loved Linette . . ." Even as I spoke the words, Nanette's open threat to Theresa came back to me and I began trembling.

"But, Linette was wearing your cape. The Commissioner has not told your grandfather that she was. The old gentleman is most agitated. His physician has been called out from Strasbourg to administer a sedative."

"But what about the other attacks? Am I to now assume that they were coincidental accidents?" The doctor on board ship told me that I was accident prone. It would be a tremendous relief if my life and grandfather's had not been in danger.

"They are still under serious consideration, Mademoiselle."

And this is a case apart, I thought, but I couldn't accept it.

CHAPTER 16

Instead of Linette waiting for me on the chaise lounge, it was Aimee, her face awash with tears, her knees apart, her hands in her lap clutching a police revolver.

Poking the gun into her pocket, she ran to lock the door behind me.

I stared in horror at the gun. I'd never seen one this close before. "Do you know how to use a gun, Aimee?"

"We were all taught during the war. The inspector asked me to sleep here. He gave me his own gun." Her smile through her tears told me she was glad that even though Jules had been taken to jail, she didn't believe he did it, nor did the police. She dropped back down on the chaise. "You already know Linette wore your cape, cherie. No, don't look like that. You couldn't have helped it. There is someone crazy here. We are to tell no one that it was you who was intended to be murdered. We are to trust no one. They have taken your cape."

I had held myself under rigid control that was no part of courage all through the long trip to Strasbourg. I had somehow managed to maintain strength when we found Antoine. But now I fell apart. Aimee drew me down beside her.

"I should never have come here. I should never have

written to grandfather. I should have stayed home and buried my father beside my mother."

"No, cherie. We can not look ahead . . ."

"But look what I have done. Because of me a fine old gentleman is dead. A young girl, innocent and sweet, is dead because of me. Her fiance's life is ruined, and he may even die. I have done all of this by writing one letter, that first letter to grandfather."

"Cherie, if you had seen him, if you had heard him when that letter came. He ran through the chateau like a boy reading it to everyone, showing everyone, telling everyone. He called all of his friends. He began ordering the dismantling of this playroom to give you your own suite, your very own. He knew months of happiness because you and your father were coming . . ."

"And then father died . . ."

"A part of your grandfather's happiness died with him, but the knowledge that you would bring him home at last to be with his own gave him still another kind of happiness. He had known no happiness after Armand left. He did not know where he was, or if he was alive. Knowing that he and Elsa had a life together and a child meant more to him than anything or any gift. You are too young now to understand that all of life has grief and sorrow. But one day when you are old you will look back upon your life. The rare hours of pure joy will stand out like stars in a black sky, and you'll gaze upon them remembering each one. For some of us, they are but few. Armand gave a great gift to your grandfather in leaving . . . Not his act of leaving, but his work in determining a way to save the wines. It was with the money your grandfather made that he was able to rebuild this little empire that to him means Laurens, the Laurens family. And, Armand gave him the gift of you, the real treasure . . ."

"But my coming has put his own life in jeopardy."

"That would not distress him. He is old. If he died, he would die happily if you were safe. And we must keep you safe."

She got up and went to the table in front of the fire. "We will have a glass of wine together, cherie. We must plan. Everything must be done to keep that one fact of Linette wearing your cape from your grandfather. Tonight his doctor has given him a sedative. Oh, and also to your Aunt Olivia who has been frightfully upset over Linette's murder."

It must be that she suspects that shot was meant for me, I thought. Aunt Olivia was astute.

I sipped the wine. "Aimee, everything that has happened has been because I came. I should leave immediately."

"What good would that do?" she scolded.

"I could renounce any claims. That would remove the motive." I clapped my hand over my mouth. I was accusing some member of the family.

She shrugged. "Don't be afraid to talk about that to me. Alphonse and I witnessed the reactions far more often than your grandfather did."

Did I dare question her about the members of the family? She had been here in the chateau, a trusted and accepted person, far longer than any of the relatives living here now.

The opportunity passed. She bustled about the room preparing my bed and her own. I heard her gasp, and walked over just as she was shoving Linette's petit point bag behind the screen . . .

I suppose it was the wines that let me sleep that night. When morning came with brilliant sunshine, I sat up. Aimee had opened the draperies, made her bed and had gone.

I had just walked to the window when I heard a key in the lock. She came in smiling, carrying two breakfast trays which she put down before returning to lock the door.

"Your grandfather is much distressed, but his health is better. His temperature has gone down. The doctor and the inspector have ordered him to stay in his suite. When you are dressed, you are to visit him. I have just come from there."

We had breakfast together at the round table far from the windows overlooking the ruins and the moat. She brought back the atmosphere of the old playroom by telling me remembered stories about father and his brothers.

Grandfather was indeed agitated. His first words to me were, "Daphne, I can't get through to Commissioner Etienne. He must release Jules immediately. That boy is no murderer. I've known him all of his life. He's a gentle, sensitive boy. He loved Antoine and he's been in love with Linette most of his life."

I put my arms around him. "It doesn't seem that he would have done it."

"Certainly not. But he had the gun in his hand. It was Antoine's, a souvenir from World War I. They never lock their houses back there. Anyone could have taken the gun."

"It would have had to be someone who knew he had it."

He looked thoughtful, and he was calming down. It helps people to talk things out, even to themselves but far better to tell someone else. He called Vallant who came in from the kitchen.

"Did Antoine have a gun, Vallant?"

"Certainly, sir. He wore it every Bastille Day. He took it off a German soldier in a battlefield on the Marne. He was very proud of it, kept it in good shape, too, oiled it and cleaned it. Showed it to all the children." Suddenly his nice eyes frowned. "You mean . . .?"

"Yes, yes, that was the gun found beside Linette."

Grandfather turned to me. "Then someone could have gone in and taken it. But why anyone would want to kill a sweet little girl like Linette . . ." Whatever he was going to say, he changed his mind. "No one can ever tell me he could stab his uncle. Yet the police say that Linette knew of their quarrel and he suspected she might give him away."

"A lot of people knew of the quarrel. It was mentioned last night at the dinner table."

"By whom?"

"Aunt Michele, I believe."

"Naturally. She slips around bowing and scraping in those soft soled shoes of hers. She sits in the dark in the door keeper's room and watches everyone. I have often wanted to tell her that's why she has pop-eyes."

I nodded. Then the pretty little green room overlooking the front courtyard was Aubert's. That chair where she found her book was her lookout. I wondered that she had not caught her own daughter slipping out to meet Jules, if that was what she did.

Grandfather was still trying to work it out. "If Jules shot her and knew where she lay, I don't believe that he could have stayed with her mother for more than an hour talking about the wedding. Linette's mother has been delaying their plans waiting for a small inheritance so she could give her girl a nice dowry."

"Dowry?"

"An old world term for whatever a bride takes with her into marriage. It is sometimes a sum of money. Most often it is a trunk of linens and silver and glassware that the mother has saved for and accumulated over the years of her child's growing up . . ."

"A hope chest."

"Yes. In Germany it is known as an aussteuer." Reaching over, he took both my hands in his. "I have hesitated to tell you this, Daphne. That letter that was lost in Paris and which I have had Vallant watching for contained a large check on a Basel, Switzerland bank. It comprised with interest your mother's aussteuer sent to me by your cousin Elsa. No one had touched the money in all those years. It touched me because I knew that the children could have often used it, have needed it, but their father was so certain that Elsa would one day come home or send for it that he made them promise not to use it ever."

"What a shame. I'm so sorry."

"The day after you told me I called the bank and had payment on the check stopped so that we do not need to worry about it. And when you meet Elsa, she need not know that it was lost. You can go to the bank with the proper identification at some future time and collect the sum, which is a tidy one."

"I shouldn't like to do it if they need it." But it would be a blessing to me. I could send it home as payment on the house. I didn't tell grandfather that, however.

"I'm sure they don't need it now. Elsa has her own

business and the boys are in the university. Besides, she would be hurt. She wrote with great pride when she sent word that she couldn't come to your father's funeral. She wanted you to have it. After all, Daphne, that was your mother's. She most certainly would have wanted you to have it."

I sat smiling and thinking about it. As soon as grandfather was well enough, I would go home. This inheritance that was in no way concerned with the Laurens' fortune would be my excuse for turning down any part of the Laurens' inheritance. Closing my eyes momentarily, I saw our small house, the dusty street, the elms and cottonwoods, my flower garden. Would I be like my father? Would I leave my home for another life? Without the stress, life in Chateau Laurens with grandfather would be wonderful . . .

"So I told Pierre . . ." Grandfather had been talking to me and I had not been listening. "I told Pierre that he might take you for a drive through the countryside so that you can better know your own country."

My heart leaped. "But Nanette? Will she go along?" I had been avoiding any thoughts of Pierre. His attraction was more than I could bear. When I did think about him, I tried to push away from it until I could go home. My hopes had been that life here would settle down enough for him to put on his coveralls and go to work in the vineyards.

A definite twinkle came into grandfather's eyes.

"I believe that your Aunt Olivia suggested that they go into Strasbourg to have their hair done, indicating that the dampness had ruined Nanette's. To put it squarely, Nanette fell for it. Whereupon Olivia suggested luncheon at the Maison Kammerzel, which

Celeste reported Nanette couldn't resist." He smiled broadly. So they were all in on it to give me an outing. He went on. "After luncheon at Olivia's suggestion also, they will visit a mutual friend who has just returned from England. This program would take Nanette away for the day while Pierre attends to his work."

His expression was bland, his cheeks working effectively to keep from laughing. The scheming old darling. I leaned forward to kiss him.

"Pierre's a good guide. I fear you shall have to travel in his sportscar. One of our cars is broken down. I placed the limousine at the disposal of the ladies. Nanette is very impressed with it and prefers it and a driver for her trips into town."

I stood up to leave.

"With the sun shining upon spring in France, put aside your mourning and all of the horror of these past few days and enjoy yourself."

CHAPTER 17

With grandfather's admonition about putting aside mourning, I chose an orchid sweater with a skirt I had made of a remnant, a classic tweed of heather. Since this was to be a sight-seeing trip, I wore grey suede walking shoes. The air blowing my curtains was cool. As I turned to pick up my cardigan, I glanced in the mirror. Color had returned to my cheeks.

Now, murder didn't seem a part of my life. Fear that had begun in Paris seemed far away. Some part of my mind was accepting that Jules had somehow been driven . . . and yet . . . No. I put it out of my mind. The sky was a clear washed blue. I was hurrying to meet Pierre. Nanette would be furious if she found out she had been tricked. I'm not usually heartless, but this delighted me. I would have one day to remember.

As I ran down the staircase I knew that part of my lightheartedness of the morning was the news of my inheritance from mother. That was surely my own and it gave me a new freedom from money worries. I needed the security of knowing I could pay for our home in Taos. I was far away in a strange country, but I had a home to return to . . .

Pierre was leaning against the stair railing watching

me come down. Catching me, he removed my dark glasses. I had become so accustomed to my black eye that I didn't bother to cover it anymore. It was now at its height.

He touched my cheek lightly. "I feel badly about that night, Daphne. It had seemed such a good idea to have a woman to comfort you on shipboard. After I met you and realized your composure, I knew you didn't need her."

My mind told me that I was reading something in his eyes that my heart wanted to find there. My mind won. It ws tenderness and sympathy, nothing else. He was so handsome, especially this morning in grey tweeds with a scarf of a bittersweet print.

His car, a red convertible, waited outside the main door in the courtyard. We drove out through the arcade of blooming chestnut trees into the main road. He pointed out grandfather's vineyards that extended for a long distance, planted vertically on the hills in hundreds and hundreds of rows of identical wooden sticks. The grape leaves in this early spring with sunshine dappling them were pale chartreuse on still wet black vines.

Pierre pointed out four large buildings. One, four stories tall and climbed over with vines, was very old and showed signs of having been repaired. The others were modern.

"That is where the wine kegs are stored, and also where I work. My offices are . . ."

I laughed.

"What's so funny?"

"Grandfather wrote that you worked with him in the vineyards. I visualized you both wearing overalls and picking grapes."

"In September we do that. When the proper time

comes, when the grapes are ripe and plump, it is not unusual for the entire family to come out and help except Theresa who has disdained such labor although her mother always joins. Most of the servants do also. It is a time of happiness, the harvesting of the grapes, a time of parties, festivities. You are going to love it."

"I can't stay until September, Pierre."

Reaching over, he patted my arm. "The problems of the chateau appear to be over now. We must forget the sorrow. It isn't easy to accept that it was Jules. I've known him since he was a boy. If he went out of his head, it was because Linette's mother has stalled their marriage for a year waiting for an inheritance. Poor children. But it is over. When your grandfather has recovered completely there are many trips planned for you. Write to your girl and ask her to stay on."

He made it sound so easy. And I could do that. In fact, with the inheritance from mother I could even close the shop until my return. Looking at Pierre, I knew that to stay on, seeing him every day, knowing the utter impossibility of my deepening feelings for him, would be agony.

I studied him in this new relaxed attitude. Was he really ready to believe that Jules was guilty? Or was he trying to lessen my fears? Whichever, he was convincing.

Traffic had picked up. While Pierre attended to his driving, I enjoyed the passing panorama of colorful villages with their vine-covered cottages, window boxes wild with colorful flowers. Ancient timbered houses leaned into each other with storks' nests on their chimney pots.

At a turn in the road I caught my first glimpse of the

black pine forests of the Vosges Mountains that I knew from scenes of father's paintings. I gasped at the view of an old castle high on a peak. Father had painted it in winter and in autumn with vivid colors standing out from the black of the pines.

"We have this whole day so we can stop wherever you wish. If you see something that attracts you, just tell me."

Either he was also ready for this outing, or he was seriously trying to please grandfather by entertaining me.

We stopped on the outskirts of Molsheim where a group of brightly dressed children celebrated some special occasion by marching with bouquets in their hands and singing.

Endless vineyards walked up the foothills of the Vosges, interspersed with houses and outbuildings, gardens and flowers, a paradise far removed from the horrors of murders. As we rode, Pierre told me the story of wine making, a history going back to the days the Romans planted vineyards along the Rhine, how wines got their distinctive character from the kind and quality of the grapes, the locality in which it is produced.

"When we get back, I'll spend a day showing you how the sparkling wines are bottled before fermentation. The noneffervescent wines are stored in vats. We have an old one as large as the entry hall at the chateau. I keep waiting to break it open and study it for leaks. And you'll love the little mice who live under the vats."

"Love mice?"

"These are special mice, very small. All of the women and children who visit feed them."

Past noon, after three stops at old ruins, we entered the city of Colmar, about fifty miles from home. Here we strolled through the delightful Venetian Quarter traveled through by the river Lauch. Men poled flower-filled boats, that were long and flat, from the wharflike porches of their homes.

"I've always wanted to see Venice."

"You shall. I promise."

I looked at him in wonder. What could he mean? My heart felt as if two small cold hands clasped it. It was at that moment that I recognized fully how deep my feelings had become for Pierre. It was unthinkable that so worldly a man would love me. Why did my first love have to be unattainable? I turned from him and looked down the river. I would not misunderstand him again. He liked me because I was a Laurens, like family to him. In so many ways, he seemed more a Laurens than any of the rest who lived with grandfather. And he loved the whole place. I knew now that the vineyards were his whole life. I could not imagine a girl like Nanette in the role of his wife.

"Father was commissioned to paint a number of scenes along the canal in San Antonio, Texas. Our hotel had a lovely wharf built out over the water. I sat there watching tourist boats. That is as close to Venice as I'll ever get."

He was standing at my side, holding my hand and looking down at our reflections. "Those heels are lower than you usually wear. You don't even come to my shoulder." He turned to measure the top of my head against his coat sleeve, then put his hand under my chin, raised my face and kissed me gently.

"I shan't let you go home, Daphne."

"Well I must." A coldness crept over me as harsh thoughts struck me suddenly. He could not seriously be considering me for his future in spite of his meaningful-sounding remarks. There could be only one answer, an answer I would never have thought of before I left home. Pierre, not a Laurens, wanted desperately to keep the business intact. With my share on his side, he could do that. I began to look upon him in a new and frightening light.

I looked back upon his contemptuous attitude when we first met on the ship. He had come prepared to dislike me, to wish I had never been, because I could stand between him and his life at Chateau Laurens. Putting myself in his place, I could understand his feelings. An American coming into an inheritance would, when her grandfather died, wish to break up the estate and return home with her share.

He was still referring to the future. "There is much of Europe that I would love to show you. And even though I can not do it now, you should travel while you are here and have someone taking care of your shop."

This was not the time to tell him that I had little money in the bank after two long expensive years of father's illness. While we walked, he talked on about cities of France that I should visit. I scarcely listened. I was telling myself that I had the strength to control my feelings, and that I would never let them show. With his good looks and charm, I knew he was used to making conquests. I would not be one of them. I hoped that I was wrong in my judgment but the fact remained that his mother helped arrange this outing by tricking

Nanette into going into Strasbourg. I knew one thing now. I was glad I had been spared the youthful love that had hurt so many of my friends.

By the time we had toured Colmar, I was convinced that it must be one of the loveliest towns in France. I would never forget our stroll through the peaceful convent gardens.

"Are you tired?"

"Thank you, no. I'm loving it."

"I told your grandfather that we were not to be expected back for dinner."

"You told him that? But what of Nanette?"

His brows drew together in a frown. I had trespassed into his private life. His tone was shockingly cruel. "Yes, what of Nanette?"

I decided not to answer. I was going to enjoy this outing. To me now, Pierre was merely a man my grandfather had chosen to show me this part of France. I took his small road map and began to study it.

"I've always wanted to see the Black Forest. We aren't awfully far from it now, are we?"

"I should have thought of that. However, Olivia and I are going to take you to visit Elsa in Freiburg, but we must make arrangements in advance. It would not do to barge in on her. You've been expecting deep black trees and undergrowth. The Black Forest is much like these in our own Vosges Mountains, not truly black."

I was delighted to know that I would meet my cousin. Visiting her would tell me if she needed mother's money. If she did, I couldn't feel right taking it. And at last I would see the real Black Forest. Pierre was right. Always my thoughts showed it as a mountainous area of solid black fir trees. Here in the Vosges were dark conifers, but of a tremendous variety and not black at all, but very dark. And not solid but growing with deciduous trees of many varieties, beech, birch, elm and a poplar that resembled our aspen at home.

We passed valleys with small farms. Little cottages with thatched roofs, all delightfully neat and flower-laden. There were whole fields of wildflowers. On one road pheasant wandered, only to flee to the sides upon our arrival. Pierre pointed out tobacco fields, mulberry orchards. There were villages of clustered three-story white houses with patterned brown or black timbers, and always the storks' nests.

By late afternoon we had reached Mulhouse, were Pierre took me to a factory, because he had noticed my interest in fine materials. Here, men and women were weaving and spinning wool. After a run through the neat city with geranium-filled window boxes, we took the Crest Road into the mountains. At a view point, Pierre stopped. He pulled binoculars from the compartment and handed them to me.

"You can see the Black Forest from here. No, aim across the river." He stood beside me, turning me. "And there is Basel. I had planned that we'd have dinner at a good spot in Mulhouse, but since this is a special day, it should be a special evening, so we'll eat in Basel."

Later we crossed the Rhine from Lesser Basel into Greater Basel, a delightful city of narrow streets with fast-moving street cars. We walked through an arcade of shops to cross a busy street. Ahead, stretching up a steep hill, waited a broad cement stairway. At each level, houses had been built with flower-filled balconies overhanging the steps. We strolled to the top where we watched the riverboats.

For dining, Pierre chose an old and famous hotel, The Three Kings on the Rhine. Women were fashionably dressed. I felt like a tourist, especially when the asparagus was served. I had already learned that in Europe new garden vegetables were treated as being very special. Here the new asparagus was more than fourteen inches long, and served on a silver platter with a frightening looking silver instrument. Much to the delight of fellow diners, Pierre got up to stand behind me to teach me how to operate it.

We had left Chateau Laurens to join The Wine Road. Since it was so late, Pierre preferred to return by the river road so that I saw the Rhine bathed in moonlight for the first time. As we rode, Pierre pointed out various places of interest. All day a little part of my mind had questioned where I had heard of Colmar. Pierre stopped about halfway between Colmar and Strasbourg to explain to me that in 1945 the Germans had launched an offensive attempt to retake Alsace.

"This is called the 'Pocket of Colmar.' American troops moved up here with the French and broke up the attack."

Of course. My father had been in one of those divisions. I couldn't believe that he had been so close to his home and had not gone there. Still, the chateau had been evacuated. If he had managed to go, no one would have been there. Poor father. There was so much in his life that he had never told me. He had been a silent man, so unlike my relatives here in France. He had not told me about his war days. I had only overheard a conversation between him and a man who had been in his division.

The chateau was dimly lit and quiet when we arrived. Pierre took me to my door, lifted my face and kissed me. I watched him walk down the hall with mixed emotions . . .

CHAPTER 18

With moonlight glinting on the gun beside her, Aimee lay sleeping. I undressed quietly and went to bed, but sleep wouldn't come. I lay pondering the two sides of Pierre. I had known no man intimately except my father. He had two sides too; perhaps we all do. Although father was often moody and pensive, he was also a willing and delightful companion. We did many things together. Right now when I was deeply troubled, we would have walked in the moonlight.

We often walked the woods, especially on fall or winter evenings, to watch for a rare phenomenon of the skies about Taos, the Sangre de Cristo Glow, a color father was to eventually capture on canvas.

Many artists had attempted to get the exact color as well as photographers, but few were fortunate enough to be on hand when this rare glow appeared. On cold winter evenings, as the last crimson line appears above the mountains, comes this fleeting transient glow, and for an instant the entire sky is pale amethyst. We often tried to describe the exact color which was neither violet nor orchid but by then it would be gone.

The first painting in which father captured the true color was of a small white adobe hut in winter. The lean-to at the front was still hung with drying red and green peppers and corn. Smoke arose from the outdoor, round, baking oven tended by an Indian woman in a bright woven skirt and shawl. I kept the painting in my shop but would never sell it. Out of it came many orders for more with that lovely sky. That was the beginning of father's small success. After that his moods had changed. Our lives became more cheerful and remained so until his illness.

These reflections gave me a little insight into Pierre's mood on the ship. He could not have helped resenting me. But remembering how father and I had been fascinated by the glow made me deeply lonely. I missed him. It would be terrible to go home and not find him there.

I stirred restlessly. The moonlight was almost as light as day. No one would be about at this hour. Flinging off the down comforter, I slipped to the closet and got my dressing gown. A brisk walk in the courtyard would let me forget, and might make me sleep.

The lights in the hall chandeliers had been turned off, but small sconces along the floor were lighted. I went down the stairs to the entry hall. I had noticed two side doors opening into the courtyard the day Aunt Olivia and I toured the chateau. The one on the clock room side had been propped open by a heavy gold dog. I chose it since I didn't have a key.

A nightingale's song soared across the night reminding me of Michael, who had stopped me hurrying home through the Tuileries to listen to one. It would be a relief to get an answer to my letter to him. It had occurred to me more than once, that I should have done something immediately when he disappeared so suddenly.

Staying under the canopy, so as not to be seen from an upstairs window, I walked swiftly in my soft slippers up and down from one end of the arcade to the other. I felt no fear, no apprehension. A light showed clearly in the gate-keeper's cottage. I have a good voice as well as the ability to whistle shrilly—the way I used to call father in to dinner when he worked in the garden.

Passing the clock room, I stopped to listen to the ticking clearly evident through thick windows and walls. The sounds might be annoying to some but were comforting to me; we had so many clocks at home. Now all stopped and waiting . . . I dropped down on the cold wrought iron bench and drew my dark robe around my legs. Stopping here brought back Antoine . . .

Antoine and Linette dead, presumably killed by young Jules who was evidently having an affair with Theresa which was very likely the cause of his quarrel with Antoine. The older man would have told him that a girl in Theresa's position could only be flirting and not serious. I was certain that Theresa would never consider marrying a poor young man however handsome.

But would Jules kill his lifetime sweetheart if she found out about Theresa? Whoever shot Linette didn't do it on the spur of the moment. It was planned. He had the gun with him. If Linette knew or suspected that Jules had killed his uncle in a fury . . . But Aimee said the inspector—I presumed she meant the commissioner—had given her his gun to protect me, intimating that he didn't really believe that Jules committed the crimes. I tried to think of Aimee's exact words. I had been completely distraught at the time.

If the commissioner wasn't entirely satisfied, why had he charged Jules with the murders? To protect him.

Perhaps he believed that Jules knew who the murderer was and was afraid to reveal his identity. It made sense that if anyone would have seen the murder, it would have been Jules who was to meet Linette out by the ruins. But he wouldn't have gone to her home to sit talking with her mother if he had seen . . . But he didn't know then that it was Linette. I couldn't make that theory stick any more than I could believe that Jules was guilty.

As I sat listening to the soothing ticking of the clocks, my mind refused to stop searching. It was all so bewildering and frightening. I wished that I could recall more clearly what Aimee told me the inspector said. Perhaps he told her there were two cases for inquiry. Certainly it had not been Jules in Paris or in Dusseldorf. But suppose the commissioner took Jules in to throw off the suspicions of the real murderer. Or to protect Jules.

Jules, closer to Antoine and Linette in life, would be more apt than anyone else to guess who might want them out of the way. And he might have seen whoever took his uncle's gun. That could have been anyone who lived or worked in the chateau, the grounds or the vineyards. If that had been the case, why would Jules hesitate to tell the police to save himself? He wouldn't . . . unless he was afraid for his own life and thought he would be safer in jail. A boy as terrified and grieved as he must have been wouldn't have been thinking clearly.

If he wasn't afraid for his own life, could he be trying to protect someone? Whom would he protect? Doubtless either someone he loved or feared. For a moment during which I didn't even hear the clocks, my mind snapped upon a shocking idea. If Antoine had threatened to expose the affair to Aunt Michele or grandfather, then Theresa . . . No. I didn't think she had that much gumption. But Aunt Michele. She had been at the door of the clock room when, or shortly before or after, Antoine had been killed. Also, she had been in grandfather's study and could have taken the jeweled knife.

I was trembling. If Aunt Michele went to the clock room expecting to find grandfather, and Antoine gave the news to her right then, she'd have been furious enough to murder him, but she would have had time to cool off by the time she went back to the study for the weapon. If anyone in the chateau knew that grandfather had not gone to the clock room for his usual day, it would have been Aunt Michele. From her vantage point in the chair in Aubert's little green room, she could have observed grandfather leaving for Strasbourg. One thing was certain, Aunt Michele would do anything to keep grandfather from finding out his granddaughter was having an affair with one of the help. With his old world ways, and his fine sense of family, he would have been horrified.

So Aunt Michele had a motive for killing Antoine and the opportunity, but why kill innocent little Linette? Could Linette have passed and seen her do it? She couldn't have seen around the L of the room, but someone passing these windows could have seen. Grandfather had been standing out here alone the night that Antoine was killed, and everyone else was inside waiting for us to arrive. But Linette was dead, and if not mistaken for me, someone planned the killing. Linette was such an emotional little thing, she would have shown the effects of such a horrible knowledge when I got here, which she did not. She was practically dancing with the joy of life and love for her Jules. Jules would not want to protect Aunt Michele, but if he was in love with the cold but beautiful Theresa, he would protect her . . .

Nothing in my life had prepared me to attempt solving crimes, or solving anything. I always took my problems to father. I believed that I would always be able to do so. I felt small and lonely in this empty courtyard, but still not sleepy. Pierre had upset me very much today. I still had that to think out.

Inside the room behind me, a number of clocks began chiming the half hour. A ship's clock struck five bells, followed instantly by the striking of many clocks. It was two-thirty. Antoine had been dead just a short time but Bertin and Monsieur Rochelle had not been able to keep all of the clocks accurate.

It wasn't right for me to think that Aunt Michele or Theresa would kill Antoine. If grandfather had not been so positive that Jules was innocent, it would be easy to accept that solution. Whom would Jules fear? What would be of vital importance to Jules with his uncle and his sweetheart both dead? His job and his home where he spent his lifetime, his security? Grandfather would be responsible for that. He wouldn't fear grandfather. But grandfather was old and frail. I suppose Caron would take his place. I wouldn't blame anyone who was afraid of Caron.

Pierre should be the one to step into grandfather's position. He loved the vineyards. And certainly he would not be one of those wanting to break up the estate. . .

I had to realize that the affair between Jules and

Theresa might be serious, that they could be planning to marry. If that were so, they would have had many obstacles to overcome. Grandfather, I felt certain, would be one of them. Obviously Antoine had objected strenuously, and he was killed. Linette would certainly have objected, and she had been killed. I could see that the Commissioner had a good case against him.

If so, Grandfather and I were safe and my incidents had been accidents. I couldn't understand why Aunt Michele, with her habits of observation, had not been aware of Theresa and Jules' affair. She was a suspicious woman, and not a pleasant one. And she was obviously in love with Caron. If ever two persons in this world deserved each other, it was Aunt Michele and Caron. On the kinder side, Aunt Michele had shown a knowledgable interest in the vineyards and the business. She knew more about Chateau Laurens than Caron.

In spite of holding Jules, I suspected that the police would arrive in numbers to make a thorough investigation. They would want to know motivations, the availability of all of us at the time of the murders. I supposed that they had special methods of determining if a person was capable of committing murder. Caron had told them in the short inquiry into Antoine's murder that he had come home early from the office the evening I arrived. He stated clearly that he had believed grandfather took his usual day in the clock room. But for me to assume that he, cold fish that he was, would want to kill grandfather when at most he had to wait for only a few years was foolish.

I had been here a very short time and had already found many undercurrents of friction and disharmony in the family. Aunt Celeste was also in love with Caron.

If she somehow managed to marry him, she would have her own inheritance from Uncle Alfred's share as well as Caron's share. From the little I had observed of her, she had no love for material things. But she was a delightful schemer as was apparent in her part of the plot to get Nanette away from Pierre to take me on a day's outing.

I wondered about that now. Could that have been an attempt to encourage Pierre's interest in me to gain my share? There wasn't any question in my mind that Aunt Michele would like to see Pierre and Theresa a team. Behind that timorous personality, and that creepy way of slipping around, there could very well be a concealed desire to get out into the world. Since she always had a book in her hand, or had one stashed somewhere, I decided to take the first opportunity to look into her reading material . . .

To my horror, I heard a gate open and close and the sound of footsteps. I was too far from the door I'd left propped open to run inside so I stuffed my feet under my dark robe and hoped I wouldn't be seen.

I was soon able to make out two tall figures walking arm in arm in the opposite arcade. They had evidently come in from the formal gardens. As they reached the arcade door across from the one I had used, the man unlocked it and pushed it open. I recognized Nanette's lovely hair glistening in the soft light.

I unashamedly watched a passionate embrace such as I'd seen in motion pictures and on television. Hand in hand, they went on into the main hall.

So Pierre had left me at my door and gone straight to Nanette. I knew now that I would sleep. I was very good at crying myself to sleep . . . I started to get up to go inside when another sound startled me. It was the gate again, but this time it had been slammed. A tall figure moved silently up the opposite arcade. In the moonlight I recognized the tilt of the curious head as she strained to look the length of the arcade to make sure the ones she had been watching had gone into the chateau. Assured, she moved silently in her soft-soled shoes to the same door, unlocked it, and stood for the moment that it took me to recognize Aunt Michele.

CHAPTER 19

The next morning I found grandfather looking much improved physically but upset with the commissioner.

"He won't give me details, Daphne, but insists that he has a firm case in spite of the fact that Jules is mighty convincing in his denial and his terrible grief."

As I poured a cup of grandfather's special and very delicious coffee blend I wondered how long it would be before the commissioner told grandfather about Theresa and Jules. That would be frightfully upsetting to him, and he was frail.

"Now sit down and drink your coffee and tell me all about yesterday." His eyes fairly twinkled. "Vallant has reported your late return."

I heard Vallant turn the key when he let me out to go downstairs to meet Robert. Grandfather said he waited in the door keeper's room to give me my French lesson. I had hoped that Pierre would be taking me on the tour through the vineyards and buildings where the wine was made. As I made the turn on the balcony to go downstairs, voices came up to me, one so strident that I stopped.

"Why must you go, Pierre?" That was Aunt Michele.

Pierre's voice was not in his normal tone and I could

imagine that this argument had been going on for some time. They were standing at the foot of the staircase. I should have turned down the corridor and gone to my room, but I simply stood there listening.

"You know that I have intended going to Paris all this week, but with events such as they have been, it was not possible for me to get away."

"Theresa is going to be bitterly disappointed. You promised her an evening at the opera. It was this special . . ."

"I'm sorry, Michele. I'll make it up to her when I return."

"If you aren't too busy driving Daphne around." There was such cold venom in the way she said my name that I shuddered.

"I don't see why you can't fly and get back in time. Nanette has made the trip often enough. She doesn't need you to escort her."

I wondered if Robert was already waiting in Aubert's room. If so, he would also be overhearing this argument.

"Look, Michele, however you feel about Nanette, you do know her circumstances. I have business in Paris. I prefer to drive. It will save her money."

At that moment, from behind me, came the snapping of heels. I turned to see Nanette ready to travel in a glorious spring green suit. With a glance at me, she leaned over the railing to look down. Her lips pursed in a half-smile and she said, caustically, "So our little pigeon is also an eavesdropper."

Since she did not know that I understood her, I smiled as if she had said good morning and answered her pleasantly as I fell into step beside her to go downstairs. I was so unnerved by the encounter that I had to hold the railing.

Pierre was standing with his hand on the railing and looking at his watch. At the sound of footsteps, he glanced up. I was almost certain that his eyes lighted when they met mine, but his goodbye was a handshake.

"I'll see you in a few days, Daphne. Look after yourself." There was heavy warning in his words and in the sober look in his eyes.

Without a word to any of us, Aunt Michele whirled on her heel and walked away just as Aimee came out of the library to usher me into Aubert's room where Robert sat with a wide but indulgent grin that creased his dark skin. "Morning, Aimee, morning, Daphne. You two just missed another of Michele's tirades at Pierre."

Aimee gave him a look of caution which he either didn't see or ignored. Strolling to the window, he watched the red convertible sweep down the courtyard to the gates.

"And so the lovers leave. On the drive to Paris they will repair the damage of yesterday."

I could only stare at him.

Relentlessly, he went on, unable to know that my heart was sore to see Pierre leave. "I came out yesterday afternoon after I finished my work thinking we would get in a lesson. The women had just returned from the city. Mademoiselle Nanette was blisteringly furious when innocently told that Pierre had gone off on a jaunt with you. She turned on both women and accused them of arranging the trip to town to get rid of her. She wanted to know if Pierre had been in on the plans. She did not come down to dinner, but had it sent up. It was quite a display of temper. And I noticed she did not speak to Pierre when she came downstairs."

Although his tale had been charmingly told, if not audacious, I made no reply.

"Have you the grammar book?"

I took it out of my purse. The walls of the room closed around me making me break out in a perspiration of claustrophobia. He was already making himself comfortable in Aunt Michele's chair.

"If you don't mind, I'd rather we worked outdoors. It is another lovely day."

He leaped up. "I'm sorry. And I offended you speaking so personally about the affairs of others. It amused me, but I should have had the sense to keep it to myself."

We walked out through the corridor that passed the clock room. My mind whirled. He must have imagined that there was constraint between Pierre and Nanette because there most certainly had not been any last night when they came in from their walk in the formal gardens.

I glanced in the clock room as we passed. Bertin, his unruly hair flying, was up on a ladder diligently wiping a tall grandfather clock. Monsieur Rochelle was not in sight. I supposed he was around the L.

Automatically, I turned away from the sight of the ruins and walked toward the cemetery. We strolled beyond the family plot. With my permission, Robert chose a wrought iron bench near a small forest of mixed trees that lay between us and the river. I sat facing the vineyards.

Robert had an expertise as a teacher. I was soon launched into verbs and making such progress that I was surprised when he looked at his watch and announced that it was time to go in for luncheon.

Throughout all of the troubles, I had maintained a healthy appetite. Placing the grammar in my purse, I joined him. Monsieur Rochelle was coming out of the clock room and walked with us.

A livid-faced Caron burst in the main door as we were passing. He stalked over to us.

"It is not enough to have all of this inconvenience of help being murdered, now Commissioner Etienne has summoned all of us to gather for another inquisition. As if any of us would harm a little mite like Linette, as if one of us might have a reason. It's ridiculous and I shall tell him so."

Alphonse, who waited at the door of the garden room, blanched at the sight of Caron and hurried to set another place.

Imperiously, Caron stood in the doorway scanning the faces of Aunt Michele and Aunt Celeste deep in conversation on one of the window seats.

"Where is Theresa? And Pierre and Nanette?"

Aunt Michele jumped to her feet. "Theresa is taking her meal in her room."

"Go get her. It is important that we hold a family conference before the commissioner gets here."

Alphonse automatically began setting another place and once again brought a chair from the side wall. Aunt Celeste walked to him with a placating expression.

"Caron, my dear, Nanette had a call from her agent who has a job for her. She is on her way to Paris with Pierre."

Instead of placating Caron, his taut face almost cracked with fury. "They should both be here. Why wasn't I called? When did Nanette's message reach her?"

"It didn't. She called the friends where she visited. They gave her the message. I fail to see any necessity for her to call you."

"I see." he said quietly. "And Pierre had an errand in Paris?"

"He said so." Aunt Celeste took her place at the end of the table.

Monsieur Rochelle, who had been studying a porcelain clock on the mantle but listening carefully to this interchange, rushed to help move her chair closer to the table and sat down at her side.

Caron sat down and picked up his wine. "I can't think what business Pierre has in Paris at this time." His eyebrows rose as he glared at Aunt Celeste.

"I don't know, Caron. He told me the night they all arrived from the ship. He said, 'I must get to Paris as soon as possible.' I didn't question him."

Aunt Olivia strolled in and a look of surprise came over her face at the sight of Caron. To me it appeared to be a look of displeasure also. Then she nodded.

"Claude just told me Commissioner Etienne was coming out with a crew of investigators. I suppose he called you, Caron?"

"Called me? He summoned me. Ordered me to get home."

Aunt Olivia patted me as she walked past. When the men were finally seated again, a flustered Aimee brought in the first course. She looked at the two empty chairs.

"I thought you were all here." She turned to go back toward the kitchens. Caron stopped her.

"Serve it, Aimee. Don't wait until it gets cold. Where is Alphonse?"

If I had been Alphonse, I would have ducked out at the first sight of Caron's face.

Aimee went on serving the plates. "He is being interrogated again by the police. He is sorry. He had hoped they wouldn't get back to him until the meal had been served."

"Get back to him? Do you mean they've been here all morning?"

She stopped to glance at him sharply. "They were here all day yesterday. I watched them from the kitchen windows. One group worked down in the ruins. Another continuously questioned the help. It has been very upsetting. The younger girls are all terrified not knowing who will be next . . ."

Caron interrupted her. "Why wasn't I informed last night?"

"I assumed you knew. There were three police vehicles parked near the garages all day."

"They were gone when I got home." He glared around the table. "Has something else been kept from me? What is this new evidence that has come up?"

Monsieur Rochelle cleared his throat nervously but continued to eat.

Throughout all of this, Theresa sat as one in a trance, the hand on her wine glass shaking. Aunt Michele ate with her protruding eyes lowered looking like bulges under her brows, her hands steady on her knife and fork as Aimee told how the police went through the home once shared by Jules and Antoine Duchamp.

I was glad I was not going to be questioned about what was served because I was so intrigued listening and watching that I paid no attention to the food.

At the end of the meal we all rose. Monsieur Rochelle bid a hasty retreat to his clock room, and it occurred to me that it was possible that some of his fellow police officers might not know that he was here under the guise of clock expert.

We gathered in the library to wait for the arrival of the police. Caron kept pouring sherry for all of us until I was sure we would be thoroughly drunk by the time they arrived. Theresa swallowed hers thirstily. She had not touched her food, and had been scolded by Aimee who interrupted herself while telling us about Linette's mother's grief and that Antoine's remains had finally been released for proper burial. She told us that Father Andre had suggested a double funeral rather than submit the entire household to two grievous affairs.

When the commissioner with his staff of three arrived, it was Aimee who suggested that they use the lovely green sitting room with the terrifying dumb waiter, that room opening off the main dining room which Aunt Olivia had shown me at a time that seemed now in the far distant past. Aunt Olivia was called first. The rest of us sat in total silence as if anything we might say would be used against us. Finally, Caron broke the silence.

"If none of you care, I should prefer to go in next. I have some pressing work at the office that must be finished this afternoon. I am sure the commissioner will understand." He didn't sound very sure of himself. His voice quavered for the first time in my presence. He looked oddly older and a bit uncertain.

Aunt Olivia came out. Caron leaped to his feet, strode to the dining room door, and disappeared. As always, Aunt Olivia was smiling and reassuring. She seated herself at my side to finish her sherry.

"There's no reason for any of us to be upset. It seems that a bit of evidence has been found with a trace of fingerprints other than Jules'. We are merely fingerprinted and requestioned about Linette the afternoon of her death."

I had been watching Theresa. She had become so pale when Aunt Olivia came out that I thought she was going to faint. As I watched, her trembling hands clasped together and she raised her head to look straight into my eyes and her white lips formed a faint smile. Suddenly, I felt deeply sorry for her. A message had come to me and been recognized; now she knew my grief for my father because she knew grief for a loved one. So she did truly love Jules. In my new knowledge of love and how much it could hurt one, I smiled at her. We sat looking at each other fully, and in my mind I chose an Indian Paint Brush bloom and said friend.

Only someone knowing what it is like to be thousands of miles away from all that has been familiar all of one's life, and to be in grief, and much of the time in terror, and at the same time to be unfortunately in love for the first time with a man completely unavailable and unattainable—could know my happiness to place a girl close to my own age on the friendship side of life. I wanted desperately to go to her, to console her, to do something to help her, but I could do none of these things now.

Aunt Olivia patted my hand. "I've a fascinating chess game on with your grandfather. And I want to assure myself that he is able to attend the funerals whenever they are held. He would insist upon attending the Mass of his old friend Antoine."

Caron came flying out of the room to stride on through without a word to anyone. Since I was sitting near the door, I saw him throw open the double main doors and go out them as if he thought someone was after him.

Aunt Celeste was called next. She was kept only a very short time, and did not return to the library. I assumed she had gone to the kitchens to consult with Aimee about meals, which was one of her assumed duties in the household. Robert Depris was called. He had been sitting quietly turning and turning his sherry glass in his hand while the other held his chin in a thoughtful pose.

I was next. As I got up I realized that Theresa and Aunt Michele were being held until the last. In passing, I touched Theresa's hand. Hers was like ice and extremely tense. She nodded, and once more gave me a faint smile that made her very beautiful indeed.

Commissioner Etienne stood up and I walked in, and asked me to sit down. Very carefully, he went over the notes he had taken when we were all questioned in the library about the time Linette was last seen alive. He put the notebook down.

"You have already been fingerprinted, Mademoiselle. Your testimony is quite clear unless you have remembered anything else."

I shook my head. "I wish I could. I'm sorry."

"Then may I assure you that we have thus far been able to keep the news that Linette wore your cape from your grandfather. The cape can not be returned to you until the case is closed." He stood up.

"Thank you, Commissisoner. I don't ever want to see it again. Linette would be alive today if I had not left it on the bench in the cemetery."

His face became stern. "No, that might be entirely wrong. We have new evidence, Mademoiselle. Please do not fret. However it is still important that you be on your guard. Stay that way until the case is closed."

As I went into the libary Theresa and her mother were waiting beside the door with one of the commissioner's men. If Aunt Michele did truly not know about Jules and Theresa I was afraid she was going to find out now.

A policeman placed himself in the dining room doorway, and nodded pleasantly at me as I picked up my purse to leave.

As I wandered down toward the clock room, the door burst open and Jeannine Villiers came running out. She came straight to me.

"Is Commissioner Etienne still here? Oh, I am so glad. I wanted my son Bertin to go in with me, but he is off somewhere." She straightened her hat. "I am going to speak for Jules. That poor boy has no one in this world now, and not one other person of the chateau has come forward."

Her heels clicked across the black and white tiles as she swept toward the library.

Monsieur Rochelle was busy with the inventory, so I walked on outside. The air was clear and soft and fragrant with flowers of spring. When I saw the activity beyond the courtyard, I turned toward the formal gardens. I had been planning to go to father's grave.

CHAPTER 20

My room did not overlook the formal gardens so I had no idea of their size. It was a veritable park, divided by the courtyard. The side where I began my walk that was to be almost fatal to me was beyond the chapel and the cemetery.

I strolled, sorely troubled, under great chestnut trees alive with chattering birds. I came upon a magnificent fountain with small marble statues of nymphs and cupids placed on the outer walls. The fountain itself, a lovely maiden holding a pitcher from which the water poured, had been damaged so that one arm was missing. Waterlilies and large, round, green leaves floated on the surface. I sat on the wall watching goldfish swim lazily, and noticing the varied patterns of the darkening clouds in shadow on the water. As shadows will, the clouds disturbed the fish making them dart into the lighter areas of the water.

A cold wind had arisen. Getting up, I walked into a topiary where hedges and evergreens had been trimmed into delightful shapes. I wandered through it, looking and marveling that someone had taken the time that must be neccessary to perform such miracles. Many of the hedges formed into deer and elk, complete with antlers, upon which small birds alighted making them move. Further into the topiary, I found an entire chess game had been trimmed of a fine-leafed privet. Underneath the grass was velvet.

It occurred to me that by continuing in the right direction—toward the Rhine, I could get into the cemetery without having to pass the courtyard where police activity had been evident. I stopped now and then to examine small circles of well-kept flowers. I don't know what I had expected in France, and I hadn't actually given much thought to anything except my grief for father so that now I realized flowers were much the same as at home. Here purple and yellow pansies had been set out. In another circle were petunias. Through a grove of slim ash, stretched a large rose garden with fresh growth on pruned bushes. Buds were forming. The earth had been freshly worked around them.

By now I had reached a tall and very thick hedge that must separate the gardens from the cemetery, but I could not find a way to pass through. I began walking the length of it moving further away from the chateau. At the end I came upon a delightful chateau that was a miniature of Chateau Laurens. As I drew nearer I recognized it as a gardener's building. Rakes and various pieces of lawn equipment lay in the courtyard.

In delight, and thinking what a perfect place it would have been for a children's playhouse, I sat down on one of the stone benches that were found in the gardens. It was pleasant there out of the wind. The oncoming storm sent birds scurrying in and out of the trees. I had thought myself alone until voices came from behind the building.

Unintentionally, I listened, but the words were muted

by the wind stirring the trees. I assumed it was two gardeners until I caught the name Claude. It seemed unlikely that gardeners would refer to grandfather in that manner. Evidently the two men were coming around the building. I caught one sentence. The voice was not distinguishable. The words didn't mean much to me.

"He has been wanting to go over the books. I must make some changes to cover the . . ."

I heard footsteps apparently entering the building. If whoever they were came on through to the small courtyard, I would be caught listening again to conversations that didn't concern me. Getting up, I moved back to the walk along the hedge to a gate that stood open as if someone had just gone out and intended to return.

Noticing that the gate had a spring lock, and fearing that the wind would blow it shut behind me, I stooped to place a rock to prop it open. I had entered the vineyards. As tall as I, the gnarled black trunks stretched into infinity. I stood gazing at the impressive sight.

A high-pitched scream was instantly followed by the crack of a rock on metal as Bertin flew out of the row of vines in front of me.

I stared in horror at the sickle on the ground beside me. Bertin's little face convulsed.

"Mademoiselle. You could have been killed." With his sling shot still gripped in his hand, he stooped to pick up the implement which had come flying over the fence.

I was too astonished to speak.

"That was thrown at you, Mademoiselle." Snatching my hand, he ran toward the gardener's house calling out angrily, "Who threw that sickle?"

We entered the house. It was unoccupied, one large

room with two Ls, holding lawn mowers and edgers. The walls were neatly hung with hoes and rakes and many ladders and tree-trimming poles, the whole reeking with fertilizers.

I stood looking down at the sickle Bertin held. It was dull looking and rusty. All of the other instruments were well-kept, oiled and clean.

"Bertin, someone was throwing it away, not throwing it at me. But your feat with that sling shot deserves praise."

"Yes, I am expert. I've been doing it all my life."

"I'm afraid my life would have ended if you hadn't been there."

"You were just lucky. It was aimed straight at you. And I heard running."

His anger and his insistence got through to me then. Just when I had hoped that terror was a thing of the past, I knew he was right. I had been seen walking from the bench. Some words I might have overheard were dangerous to whomever was speaking.

"Let's go tell the police."

"Mademoiselle, they have gone. That is the reason I was returning to the clocks. I had to hide from them and was making good use of my time. My mother assured you that I shot stones into the Rhine. I do in season. This time of year and through summer while the grapes are ripening, it is I who keep the birds from eating them. I have saved many a crop for Monsieur Claude. When Monsieur Caron becomes the master, I shall resign."

For all of his youthful pomposity, he became slightly embarrassed. "I was not hired for the job, Mademoiselle. When very young I would see the blackbirds eating the grapes . . ."

We had reached the clock room. Holding the sickle, Bertin asked Monsieur Rochelle to call the police.

Rising, Monsieur Rochelle took the sickle with the cloth he had been using to clean a clock. He listened as we each told him our stories.

"But neither of you saw anyone?"

We both shook our heads. I had already told him I'd overheard two persons talking and assumed they were gardeners. Placing the sickle still wrapped in the cloth under the couch, he left to examine the grounds and see the gate keeper. I worked with Bertin until tea time.

To my delight, grandfather, fully dressed but looking pale and weak, came down in the elevator with Aunt Olivia.

"The doctor told me to try out my legs since I insist upon going to the services tomorrow. Father Andre has agreed that it would be easier for all if a joint funeral were held."

Aimee came in with one of grandfather's favorites, a kugelhof, a cake, baked in a designed mold, to which his own brandy soaked raisins were added. I had learned that raisins made up part of the estate income.

She exclaimed happily when she saw grandfather. "How nice. I've just sent one of these up to you."

"Vallant will take care of it."

Alphonse followed Aimee with the big silver tray laden with tea and coffee pots. He was clearly pleased at not finding Caron in charge, and bustled about happily serving us, building up the fire and placing a woven lap robe over grandfather's legs.

Aunt Celeste came. It was a cosy pleasant tea. Aunt Michele and Theresa did not appear, nor did Robert or Caron. We were listening to Aunt Olivia's account of the chess game in progress when the outside knocker on the main doors was banged impatiently. From my chair facing the hall I watched Aubert open the doors to a windblown Nanette and a taxi driver with her now familiar cases.

At the sound of her voice ordering Aubert to close the doors because the wind was ruining her hair, Aunt Celeste ran out expectantly.

"But where is Pierre? Isn't he with you?"

Nanette paid the driver. "I haven't seen him since he dropped me at my flat. What is going on here? The commissioner ordered me to return."

Aunt Celeste placed her hand on the back of her neck, an action I had noticed when she was disturbed. "But we've heard nothing from him. He didn't tell any of us where he was going. Did he leave Paris?"

"He simply informed me that he had business in Paris."

"Then I am sure we will hear from him soon. Certainly if the commissioner called you back it means an inquiry at some time after the funerals which have been planned for tomorrow."

"I can't imagine why I should have to be here for that."

They had reached the library. Aunt Celeste urged her inside. "Come in and get dry and have a hot beverage. You're shivering."

Nanette greeted us and accepted a cup of coffee from Aimee. She turned to grandfather. "It is a good thing that I was not on a long job. The one I went in for was a special showing of gowns. My next steady work won't begin until the fall showings."

This was a familiar topic of her conversations usually

aimed at the closest male. She seemed to have little to say to women. Aimee gave Aunt Celeste an interesting raised eyebrow look which was answered with a shrug as Nanette finished her coffee and stood up.

"Please excuse me. I must rest, and I have telephone calls to make. Aimee, am I to have my usual suite?"

"It is ready as always, Mademoiselle."

Nanette thanked her and walked to the elevator in that way models walk that made me watch in envy. She was so very attractive that her company always made me uncomfortable. After the elevator rose with its groans and grumblings, Aunt Olivia resumed her story and I sat back in a warm glow. Pierre had not been in Paris with Nanette all of this time that I had missed him.

Aubert came in with the afternoon post and handed me a stack of mail. Grandfather's eyes lighted at the sight of a familiar orchid envelope sticking out from the rest. I looked at it anxiously. It was not his letter forwarded as we had both hoped, but my letter returned from Heidelberg with a printed notice that no such person had been found at the university. I showed it to him and excused myself to read my mail. His anxiety sent me hurrying to find Monsieur Rochelle to ask him not to let grandfather know about the incident with the thrown sickle.

Bertin was diligently winding clocks from his ladder. Monsieur Rochelle was not there.

A letter from my friend June in Taos, told that she was happy to continue running the shop. All was going well. She had carried out grandfather's request that no more of father's paintings be sold and had taken them to my home and placed them in the hall. As I read, I could see the little house, quiet and lonely, on the dusty street, shadowed by the cottonwood trees. I knew in that few moments exactly how I would feel upon my return. I had become so fond of grandfather that leaving him would be quite as painful as parting with father in the old days before he took me with him on his trips. Also, I was becoming content in the chateau.

Outside, the threatening storm swept in with wild streaks of lightning and thunder that shook everything in the room. I switched on a lamp and closed the windows and returned to the mail.

June's letter reminded me once again that I should give grandfather the three paintings I brought with me. Every morning upon awakening I promised myself that as soon as he was stronger, I would do so. Getting them out of the closet, I unwrapped them and stood back in shock. Father had indeed come here during the war. How terrible it must have been for him to see the chateau in ruins and everyone gone as he had depicted it in one of the scenes. A fierce streak of lightning cracked the sky and as a clap of thunder shook the building, my light went out. There were candles in the room, and matches at the mantle. Making my way there, I lighted one and carried it to my dressing room.

When traveling, I always carried a small pocket flashlight. I removed it from a dressing room drawer and put it in my purse. If the lights were still out at dinner time, I could use it to find my way down the stairs. The elevator would be out of commission.

I sat for a long time at the window watching the storm. We had wild ones at home. Often on winter nights, they were harbingers of snow. I saw our little home in snow with the warmth of the pink glow of incandescent lights streaming from the windows. How I used to love to come home to it at early dark after I closed the shop, home to father. It was at this hour of the day that I missed him and home. Often as I sat with the others down in the libary, I would look into the fire and imagine myself opening the gate and running in to fling open the door and call out, "Father, I sold one today."

"How much did you get for it?"

"A million dollars, but it was worth more than that."

He would catch me and swing me around. "Good, that will just about pay our taxes."

They were gone, those days, those evenings, those nights we shared. They would never be again . . .

I drew the shades on the storm and pulled the draperies. Would I regret bringing him here so far from where I would spend the rest of my life? We had made a weekly trip to the cemetery where mother was buried to place flowers. Sometimes a memory would come to him. We would sit down while he told me . . .

The lights were still off when time came to go down for dinner. Drawing my flashlight from my purse, I opened the door. Small brass lanterns had been placed at intervals along the corridor.

As I walked toward the balcony Nanette came out of one of the corridors, looked down another and while running, exclaimed, "Oh, my darling, I was distressed when you were not in your office. I called three times."

"I spent most of the afternoon working in the vineyard office."

Stepping forward a few feet, I stared at Caron and Nanette in a fierce embrace. Softly, I tiptoed back toward my room.

"How did you arrange for me to come back so soon? I shall be grateful for the day when we don't have to arrange to meet."

"It was easy this time. When the commissioner called me to tell me we were to have another inquisition, I told him I supposed he would want everyone who had been in the chateau at the times of the murders. When he agreed, I gave him your telephone number and address."

"If you knew I was here, why didn't you come to me during the storm? I was frightened."

And I was horrified to know that Nanette would do such a cruel thing to Pierre. To come here to his home and carry on with another man . . .

As we dined by candlelight, the storm continued to rage. Conversation was about the storm and the grapes, and amounted to Caron roaring down the table to answer Aunt Michele's questions. Theresa did not appear, nor did grandfather. Nanette gave all of her attention to Robert as she described her recent appearance at the gown showing in Paris.

After dinner I walked to the clock room with Monsieur Rochelle. I asked him to low-key the sickle incident.

"That's true. Your grandfather shouldn't be worried until we know something definite. I've had the sickle sent into headquarters for fingerprinting. Also, I warned Bertin not to talk about it. He was disappointed that he couldn't brag about his expert shot so I told him he could help solve the mystery better by staying alert and silent."

Before retiring, Aimee and I visited grandfather's room and found Aunt Olivia concentrating on a move at the chess board. The game had resumed immediately after dinner. She was wise to keep grandfather occupied. Tomorrow would be hard on him.

The lights had not come on when we went to bed. I lay listening to the storm and to the soft sound of Aimee sleeping. My mind traced a pattern of the day, and I shivered in horror at the memory of that sickle. What if Bertin had not been there? Above the fury of the storm came the rumbling of the elevator, and the click of the lock, then the careful closing of the door. I sat straight up in bed trying to remember if Aimee had locked the door. Creeping out of bed, I went to the door and tried the knob.

"What is it, Daphne?" Aimee asked sleepily.

"The electricity must be back on. I heard the elevator."

She flicked on her lamp, and sat on the edge of the lounge. "And the storm's dying out. Your grandfather has been afraid that more rain will cause mildew in the vineyards."

"Can it be controlled?" I was to wish that I had not asked that question which brought back the miniature chateau and the implements there.

"The whole Rhine will soon smell of sulphur as the machines start dusting the vines. Now you must get to bed, Daphne. You look like a ghost. I wish you would speak to the doctor who could give you a sleeping potion."

The doctor on the ship had given me pills that night in Dusseldorf. "I think I have some."

The pills were in my purse. I had never taken medicine for my nerves, and I decided against it tonight, and chose instead to pour us each a glass of wine. Outside in the corridor we heard a trundling of wheels which Aimee said was the cart Aubert used to remove the lanterns from the corridors.

CHAPTER 21

Aimee was up at dawn, bustling about, getting ready to help the women prepare a meal for guests after the early Mass and before the police would arrive for another inquiry. Men below in the courtyard swept up leaves and broken branches, all that remained of last night's storm. I took my tray to the window. Wisps of smoke rose up from passing ships on the Rhine. I dreaded the Mass for Antoine and Linette so much that my nerves were in tatters.

I had just finished dressing when Aunt Olivia came in—as always perfectly composed, delightfully groomed and smiling.

"Here, let me help you fasten that." I'd been trying to close the clasp on my watch strap.

"It's broken. Put it in your purse. We'll get it repaired in Strasbourg. I knew that would perk you up. Claude suggested it last night when he noticed how taut you were. He cleared with Commissioner Etienne that we were not needed at the inquiry so he ordered the limousine for us immediately after the services. He has been frightfully concerned about these happenings and is most determined that the police come to a conclusion soon. And he worries about you."

All the way to the chapel she chattered about places we would visit after a sightseeing tour through the city.

Just before the Mass began, grandfather escorted Jules and the commissioner into a pew at the rear of the church. As they passed us, I could easily understand why grandfather and most of the people of the chateau couldn't believe Jules had killed anyone, let alone his beloved uncle and his sweetheart. His tragic face with great expressive black eyes was as finely chiseled as a statue's. With a sensitive mouth, black curly hair as unruly as Bertin's, he was extraordinarily attractive. I could see why Theresa could fall in love with him. There was character in his features and in his bearing. I liked the way he held his face in control although his eyes streamed tears at the sight of the two caskets at the front of the chapel. As we came down the aisle toward the family pew, grandfather placed a consoling hand on the boy's shoulder.

There was much weeping throughout the service. Aunt Olivia ushered me out a side door, and rapidly across the courtyard, the instant Father Andre finished the Mass. Grandfather had asked her to keep me from the graveside service, she told me. He had been urging the commissioner to bring Jules.

As the gatekeeper threw open the gates for the car to pass through, a crowd of photographers surged forward and were ordered back by two uniformed police. Our avenue of trees was lined with cars and police vehicles. I had given no thought to publicity. Now and then I heard radios and televisions in the chateau and in the buildings beyond the courtyard, but the television set in the library had not been turned on since my arrival.

Gratefully, I leaned back to listen to the delightful

flow of Aunt Olivia's account of Strasbourg which, she told me, had been heavily bombed by the Allies in 1944 and of course evacuated at that time. As a consequence, I was to see much modern structure as well as old buildings.

At a rise on the road, she had the driver stop to allow me a better view of the city. Dominated by the magnificent spire of the old Gothic cathedral, a portion of the city was cut off like an island by the two branches of the river Ill. Even at this distance I could see great modern buildings and small red and blue roofs of older structures.

Aunt Olivia hurried the driver along the route so that we could reach the cathedral before noon for me to see the famous astronomical clock performing. The cathedral had been built of the same native pink stone as the chateau.

Afterward, we strolled the medieval streets, among great timbered houses, to have a late luncheon at a sidewalk cafe that specialized in choucroute garni a l' Alsacienne, sauerkraut cooked with smoked loin of pork, knockwurst, and bacon—a favorite dish of hers that she couldn't teach her British cook to prepare properly. Much of the food served in Strasbourg is German, since the city has been in and out of French and German rule through centuries of its history.

We strolled through shops where I bought stockings. With the loss of my cape and my London Fog mended, I needed a new wrap. Aunt Olivia accepted this announcement with delight. An indefatigable shopper, she rushed me through stores until we found a shop that specialized in small sizes. There I bought a perfect three-piece tweed suit, skirt, jacket and matching topcoat.

The driver met us at a charming square named Marche-aux Cochons-de-Lait, the Suckling Pigs Market. After depositing my purchases in the trunk, we strolled through the neighborhood.

The afternoon and evening drive took us into the valley of the Zorn and into Lorraine. At this point, she drew from her purse a folded piece of grandfather's stationery on which a map lettered in his handwriting had been drawn. Her light attitude tightened into attention as she leaned forward to ask the driver for his roadmap. Removing a small square magnifying glass from her purse, she studied both maps, made a large X on the driver's map and handed it back to him with such a rapid spurt of French that I caught only a few words.

Still in her rather tense attitude, she turned to me. "I have an errand for your grandfather, Daphne. Then we shall continue this trip. The scenery is the loveliest in all of France."

The driver stopped the car on the side of a lovely sprawling stretch of wood and opened the map she had given back to him.

"Oh, do let us get out here. I want you to see this waterfall. Driver, we'd like to get out here for a moment."

"Certainly, Madam." Swinging out his door, he opened the one on my side. I had not looked closely at him before. I had seen the back of his head as we drove along, of course, but after the services I had been so distraught that I had not even glanced at him as we got into the car. At the cathedral Aunt Olivia had hurried me along so as not to miss the striking of the clock. Now as I stepped from the car, my heel caught in the carpeting and I fell forward. As he caught me, my hand flew out to his shoulder and clamped upon a large pistol. In surprise, I looked into his face.

With a shudder of terror, I knew that he was not one of grandfather's servants. He had not been on the stairs the night of my arrival. He was not one of the men I had seen working on the broken down car in the garages. He was a total stranger and a formidable looking one with a stern face, bright light blue eyes that did not smile when he smiled at me as he placed me on the ground.

He said very softly, "Mademoiselle is no heavier than my ten year old daughter."

Aunt Olivia followed me out, and began pointing out various scenic spots. My hands had turned to ice.

When we returned to the car he had drawn the shades in the back seat. These were like small venetian blinds through which the sun can't penetrate, no one can see in, but one can see out. I looked in frightened askance at Aunt Olivia, who patted my knee.

"That is thoughtful of the driver. Sun is hard on hair coloring. I prefer they remain closed."

I supposed she knew what she was doing, but I intended at the first opportunity to tell her about the gun. He could very well be kidnapping us.

We proceeded down a little-traveled road that allowed a fabulous view of far mountains, and which swept through meadows of flowers. The driver referred to the map, then turned into a small narrow road through a much-neglected vineyard. On each side of the car ghostly grey sticks and gnarled grape stumps, with eerie dead vines straggling in the breeze, begged for life. Recent rains had brought out new greenery that left a sheen through which sunlight filtered.

Aunt Olivia leaned forward watching with rapid glances on both sides. Her interest was intent and her hands gripping the back of the front seat turned white at the knuckles. I couldn't understand what she looked for nor what drew her attention until we passed a row separated by abandoned grape wagons like those I had seen in our own vineyards. She nodded her head at the sight of apparent activity. The earth had been plowed deeply. Pipes for irrigation stretched the length of the vineyard ahead.

The driver slowed the car as we neared a chateau with many outbuildings. Recent evidence of considerable repairs to the chateau accounted for the equipment stacked in the courtyard although there were no workmen in sight at this time of evening.

Aunt Olivia let out a soft gasp and I turned to see the rear end of a red convertible sticking out of one of the garages. At a rapid command from Aunt Olivia, the driver threw the big limousine into reverse and swiftly into what father used to call a getaway turn practised on our mountain roads by young daring drivers. At high speed we tore through the ghost vineyards.

I thought that I had seen Pierre's red car back there. Of course there were many red sportcars. I didn't know what errand Aunt Olivia was making for grandfather, but my heart felt sick to think that Pierre might be involved. If this had not been so, and that was Pierre's car, she would have wanted to see him. He had been gone for days without calling or writing to his mother who wandered about the chateau attending to her work in a perpetual state of worry. Not once in all my searching for motivations among the relatives did I considered him guilty of anything more than flirting with me to please grandfather or Aunt Celeste. I was not going to be given an explanation, and my heart would ache until I knew . . .

Forgetting about her hair coloring, Aunt Olivia raised her shade to watch along the road for an attractive cafe for tea. She chose an old, white-washed building climbed over with vines. The driver walked with us around to a side patio where tables had been placed overlooking a splendid view. He took a table some distance from ours and sat smoking a cigarette and sipping a beer.

Throughout the rest of the trip, Aunt Olivia seemed pleased. She had returned the folded orchid map to her purse, and evidently considered her mission accomplished because she began telling me the history of places of interest we passed. Even though it was all fascinatingly new to me, my mind was so busy searching for explanations that I remembered little of Lorraine as we drove back down the chestnut tree, lined road into Chateau Laurens.

The gatekeeper saluted our driver with military attention. To my surprise, Aubert met us at the car, and after my packages had been removed from the trunk, the driver, carrying them, escorted us to my room where he and Aunt Olivia deposited me and left, evidently to report to grandfather whatever they had learned on the mission.

All the while I dressed for dinner I worried about Pierre's part in the mysterious proceedings of the late afternoon. In swift determination I fastened my repaired watch strap and started for grandfather's room. By this time Aunt Olivia would be dressing for dinner and the driver gone.

But the driver was not gone, Vallant informed me at the door. I was turning to leave when grandfather's voice called out to me to come in. He was looking quite pleased although deep lines of concern showed around his eyes.

"Daphne, I want you to meet an old friend, Inspector Daladier of the Paris detective force."

I nodded to our driver of the day. He was standing at the window and holding a glass of brandy.

"Inspector Daladier once lived here and worked in the vineyards. As you know, I've not liked having our local police entering closely into family affairs until I know more about them. I called him to come as a personal favor. He is not interfering with the commissioner's fine investigation but is following an idea of mine."

His intelligent old eyes met mine steadily. "Now run along to dinner. They will be waiting for you. Tomorrow your Aunt Olivia will have a surprise for you."

I kissed him and dutifully left with all of my questions unanswered . . .

CHAPTER 22

Aunt Olivia had not kept her surprise until morning, but hd told me in the elevator on our way to our rooms after dinner. I had looked forward to meeting my cousin Elsa ever since Pierre told me that he and Aunt Olivia would take me to Freiburg. With Pierre still away, it was Aubert who would drive. His home is in Waldkirch. He would go there to visit his brother while we were with Elsa.

I had been told that Elsa resembled mother whom I had never seen except in snapshots and two portraits father painted. Her face was oval as was mine, her hair dark and shoulder length. Her most outstanding features were her slim nose and large expressive eyes.

Aunt Olivia came early to my room and had breakfast with me while we decided that I should wear my new tweeds with the blouse I had made.

Last night I had tried to decide if grandfather had recuperated enough to see the paintings that had shocked me when I unwrapped them. He would know that father had come home to the chateau after the battle in the Pocket of Colmar, had seen, and later painted the chateau in its destroyed condition. I worried about how that would affect grandfather. It would have been different if father had brought the paintings as he planned.

Father had painted our beautiful Sangre de Cristo

Glow into the sky above the bombed chateau. I thought it his greatest work. Certainly it incorporated his love for both France and New Mexico. The second painting was the chateau as he had always wanted it restored from earlier destruction. Grandfather would have known father's desires because he had restored it exactly as father painted it. The third scene of the old winery building in spring was light and lovely.

I carred them to grandfather's suite. Vallant followed me and placed each painting on a chair for grandfather to view.

He looked first at the wartorn scene. His hand flew to his mouth and he started shaking his head. "Armand did come home. He did try to find us. Poor Armand. How shocked he must have been." He held a hand out to me. "Let me study them alone, Daphne. Go along with your Aunt Olivia, and be sure to give my love to Elsa. I would like to have her come for a visit."

Aunt Olivia had called Elsa last night to make sure that our visit wouldn't interfere with her classes. I was disappointed that the boys would not be home. Elsa and her twin brother Louis were twenty-eight, the oldest, Frederich, was twenty-nine.

Part of my excitement was due to the fact that Freiburg lay in the Black Forest, actually in the most southern section. Yet, on this clear and beautiful Rhine spring day, a feeling of premonition crept over me.

As we crossed over the bridge in Strasbourg, and I looked back at the magnificent cathedral of the same rose pink stone as the chateau, I tried to throw off dark feelings. Aunt Olivia was anxious to see Elsa of whom she was fond, and chatted lightly about her and her brothers.

From the bridge we turned into the little city of Kehl, with its modern hotels mixed with what was left of the original buildings after the war. Driving through the countryside, I was again impressed with the German neatness and cleanliness that had been so evident on our trip up the Rhine.

Aunt Olivia and Aubert kept up a constant argument about which mountain was the one we could now see. One thing I had learned since I came to France was that no matter what was one's station in life his opinion was as valuable as the next man's. A servant can express and even argue his opinion with his employer without concern. The French respect each other's opinions and evidently they all love to argue. At the chateau I had become accustomed to hearing arguments about politics, the heavy rains and the probable effect on the grapes, to the naming of babies Father Andre baptized. They would argue that the food was cold or was not cold, that the curtains in the garden room should be drawn open or left closed. Caron was the most outspoken. After the arguments there were never any hard feelings.

Aunt Olivia usually remained aloof in the small family quarrels and devoted herself to stories about her amusing late husband's remarks about Parliament, her frightening flight in the storm from South Africa, and about her life in London. She often expressed the wish that I would go to London for a visit, or if I still insisted upon going home, she would travel with me. But she warned me that I could not go on until I had seen England and the rest of the British Isles. I had always wanted to see London.

Along the road we traveled, stood enchanting houses with tall peaked roofs, balconies, all colorfully decorated, and often situated in a lovely green valley or high on a wooded hill. Mountainsides were dotted with them. We passed through picturesque villages with great vineyards trailing up the mountains. At Offenberg we stopped for a delicious pastry at a cafe where Aubert had worked as a boy. We were warmly welcomed and invited to be guests of the house for a special dinner on our return trip. I was so fascinated with Aubert's friends and the city that I hoped Aunt Olivia considered our returning.

More friends of Aubert gathered. Aunt Olivia suggested that we stroll through the lovely area of the one free imperial town.

"You are going to like Elsa. She is a special person."

"You all are and I'm lucky to have you."

"I can't imagine Armand not letting us know where he was. He was always closer to his father than the other boys."

"He never told me anything about his people or mother's until his illness. Now that I know you all, I can't understand why he made such a clean break. I know he loved grandfather. I'm sure he must have loved his mother and brothers."

"Yes, and they all adored him. It was not your grandfather who objected so strenuously to your father marrying Elsa. It was your grandmother. All of her people had been killed by German bombing in World War I. Her property was confiscated and later destroyed. She got away with only her life. She was caught and brutally attacked and left for dead by a outlaw band of soldiers.

There are some in every war. A farmer found her and took her home to his family who nursed her back to health. She learned to sew and eventually moved to Paris to work for a designer from Strasbourg. She met your grandfather at one of the parties the designer held. They fell madly in love. At that time Strasbourg was under German rule. Before she agreed to marry him, she told him her full story and of her bitterness toward Germans and everything German. Think back to the bitterness and hatred in your own country after the Civil War. It was much the same here. Particularly, in Alsace."

"Yet she agreed to live at Chateau Laurens?"

"Love does strange and wonderful things to people, and terrible things. Look at your father. He grew up knowing of this hatred; it was drilled into all the boys, yet he loved Elsa from the moment they met. There could have been no one else for him. I believe they would have gone away even if the war had not come. Poor children. They were very young. They would have had little chance for happiness at home."

I was grateful for her story. I could understand now why father had felt he could never come home. He did not know that his mother was dead. And I was half German. Time is a great mender. Looking back to my trip with Aunt Olivia into Strasbourg I marveled at the blending of French and German customs and at the harmony so apparent.

Along the road we traveled were many health spas. It was not unusual to pass groups of men and women costumed and using walking sticks. I could also now understand why Pierre had laughed at me for wanting to buy my cuckoo clock before reaching this part of the Rhine. They were everywhere I looked, in every shop window we passed.

As Pierre had explained, the Black Forest was not really black, but I was enchanted. Most of it that we went through looked like well-kept parks. The hills and mountains had so little underbrush that we occasionally glimpsed a deer feeding.

As we drove closer to Freiburg the mountains were higher. At one point Aubert named one of the peaks soaring above the rest, Schauinsland Mountain. He suggested that we might go there after our visit with Elsa if we were not planning to return for dinner at his old inn.

We were passing through an area of delightful mountain chalets with peaked roofs, beautiful green valleys and open fields of wild flowers. Had it not been for the architecture of the buildings we could have been traveling anywhere in the Appalachian area back home, because these mountains were roundtops with similar shapes, and abudant with varied trees and wild life.

Aunt Olivia leaned toward me. "Has Claude told you that Elsa is an invalid?"

"No. He explained that she couldn't travel to father's funeral because of ill health."

"You won't be sorry for her. I just preferred that you not be surprised to find her in a wheel chair. You will admire her greatly. She has put herself through the university and has become one of the best linguists of the area. She could easily accept a position at the university here or at any other but she prefers to remain in her home where she teaches classes in English, French and Spanish. She is often called upon to give crash courses to young people in the diplomatic circles."

"She must be brilliant. I still have trouble with my French."

"You've done very well. But if you spent a few weeks with Elsa, you would be speaking fluently. Elsa, except for her deformity of birth, is beautiful. She has overcome a lot of her former embarrassment." She glanced around. "We are almost to Freiburg. It was severely damaged during the war, but the natives wisely rebuilt along the lines of their old architecture. In many places you can't tell the old from the new. I've been bitterly disappointed that so many cities put up these horrible metal buildings instead of attempting a true restoration. You can tell that I am one who gets out and fights to preserve many of London's landmarks."

We entered the city proper at the exact moment that deep-toned bells all over the area were ringing. A lovely sound that I would long remember in conjunction with the memory of a jolting and terrifying shock . . .

Aubert began to point out buildings of note, and I was turning right and left to see the red Kaufhous, many three and four story buildings with their steep sloping roofs and their delightful colors. The cathedral in the great square was fantastically medieval with spiked spires. In the square, a market had been set up with colorful umbrellas over the small stalls. We walked from the car into the area for a better look at the cathedral, but we didn't go inside because we were expected at Elsa's and did not want to be late.

We left to drive up into the hills against which the city rested, a spot of great beauty with a spectacular view.

Aubert drove skillfully upon a narrow twisting road through a forest of dark fir and pine to take a final steep turn into a clearing. From the window the view of Freiburg was breathtaking. Getting out, I stood gazing with delight upon a large two-story log house with a balcony across the front, and the usual high-peaked roof. The trim, against the logs, was a blue and the shutters white. We walked up steps cut from the whole trees on to a finely polished pegged wooden porch up to double white doors.

The doors were flung open by a smiling large woman in a sparkling white apron and cap. She tossed a happy greeting to Aubert who left to go to his brother's home.

When Aunt Olivia recovered her breath after a loving embrace, she introduced me to Hulda who took my hand to drag me into a hall fragrant of pine. Walls and floors and doors and every piece of furniture, the staircase ahead of us, the window frames and sills, had been made of pine and polished until the whole shone like gold.

The huge room we entered was so delightful that I simply stood taking it all in. Windows extending the full length of the room gave a spectacular view of the city and surrounding hills. A tremendous stone fireplace stood at one end of the room. The furnishings were all pine and beautifully made. The curtains and seat coverings were of a fine monkscloth, that woven white material so rarely seen today. Wide borders had been stitched in reds and oranges, with greens and blues depicting children walking hand in hand. I expressed my pleasure and lifted one curtain to examine the fine stitches.

"Elsa made them, did all of that cross-stitching. It took her two years. She has since done them for the whole house, each room in a different design."

"I've never seen anything so perfect as they are for this lovely house."

"They worked hard, those poor children." She drew me to an end window and pointed upmountain where ruins of an old chateau stood near the top. "Their home was destroyed before they were born. Your uncle made a home for them in the least damaged wing. They grew up there. Gradually, as the government made reparations for war damage, he started this house. Lewis and Frederich finished it for Elsa. They maintain residence in that same old wing of the chateau. They made all of the furnishings from their own trees felled by their own labor."

I heard a faint chuckle behind me and turned.

"Hulda. You will have Daphne believing my brothers are supermen." She held out her hands to me, and smiled.

I stared down at Elsa, certain, back in my mind, that someone had described her to me. Her face was oval like mine. Her eyes, dark and sad looking, showed her tragic pain. Her black hair was drawn back into a handsome chignon.

"You look so much like me that I'm going to let my hair grow and wear it that way."

By now Aunt Olivia was leaning over and hugging Elsa. Elsa winked at me over her shoulder.

"I hope you are hungry. Hulda has probably prepared all of her specialties."

How totally unlike my introduction to my French relatives this was. In less than minutes Elsa and I were talking about our mutual interest in fine materials, about our sewing projects and finally about mother whose girlhood pictures she promised to share with me.

Aunt Olivia had disappeared with Hulda. By the time they came back, Elsa had wheeled her chair to the windows and was pointing out various buildings in the city far below, the fine old university where she had studied, and the spires of the cathedral. Hulda carried a tray holding tall-stemmed glasses of a schnaps distilled from cherries, a fresh tasting beverage called Kirschwasser.

The highly-polished pine dining table had been dotted with mats matching the curtains. Hulda served a thick oxtail soup delicious with finely chopped vegetables and dotted with small dumplings. Then fresh mountain trout served with a light salad of chopped parsley, tomatoes and mixed fruit. At each place a freshly baked loaf of black pumpernickel waited, wrapped in white linen napkins, and tall steins of dark beer. When I thought I could not eat another bite, Hulda carried in a Black Forest chocolate cake. This she served with vanilla ice cream topped with cherries in kirsch.

While Aunt Olivia helped Hulda clean up, Elsa took me on a tour through this floor of the house. Her huge study where she held classes also overlooked the city. Bookshelves lined the walls beyond tables and work benches.

When we got to the kitchens Hulda took over to show me the cupboard doors Elsa had painted light blue with small designs of the same running children. Afterward, Hulda placed herself behind the wheel chair which she pushed down the hall to an elevator.

"My brothers built this for me. They kept insisting that it be enclosed but I prefer this way. I was always afraid of running through a glass door." I felt sure there was no other elevator like it in the world. Sturdy boards fastened with pegs were set around the cage allowing a view of the house as we ascended.

The upper floor, in the same plan as the lower, held two large guest bedrooms, a sewing room and Elsa's bedroom directly above the living room and with a similar fireplace. The monkscloth curtains in each room had different designs. I couldn't help exclaiming over them.

"I'll ship you enough of the cloth to do it for your home. Tell me about your home. I have seen pictures of New Mexico. It looks big and beautiful and varied."

It was all of that. I described the Indian pueblos, and told her that I would have an Indian friend design my curtains which I would stitch.

"It will probably take me the rest of my life because I run a shop." When I had told her that I had to get home before too long to relieve the friend who was tending it for me, she seemed disappointed.

"But you must stay. You must come back here for the celebration at Octoberfest." She grabbed my hands. "I was not going to tell you yet, but I am to marry then. I want my own cousin for my bridesmaid."

Aunt Olivia gasped with delight. "Elsa, I am so happy for you. Why haven't you written about it?"

Elsa's face held a look of dismay. "My fiance wants to wait until he finishes a book he is writing, or rather translating for a professor in Paris. He was a student at the university with me." Her head lowered so that we could not see the tears that had welled up in her eyes. "And I am still hesitant to marry. Frederich vows there is still hope that an operation on my back will . .

The rest of her words were lost to me. Her explanation to Aunt Olivia was detailed. Her oldest brother

Frederich was a medical student at Heidelberg specializing in surgery. Both boys were taking classes at the Sorbonne in Paris.

In a daze of bewilderment, I looked with a delighted Aunt Olivia, at beautiful gowns and linens Elsa drew from her long pine aussteuer, articles she had made in the years since marriage had finally seemed a possiblity to her. The happiness that flickered now and then on her serious little face made my heart heavy.

I could not keep my hands from shaking when she opened an old dark cabinet to draw out the pictures of mother and of her family.

With tears blinding my eyes I looked at pictures of mother in childhood, girlhood, happy joyous pictures that Elsa divided with me. She placed them in a manila envelope, and began drawing out more recent pictures. Louis, her twin, was exceedingly handsome with her same dark coloring. I did not need to look at the picture she held out to me of her other brother, Frederich Michael Weill. I knew that serious face and very well.

I made some comments. I don't know what I said. Elsa was chattering about the wedding. "You will meet the boys then, unless they can get away for a visit sooner, in which case I will call you to come over. You will come, won't you?"

Aunt Olivia, who had now drawn back and was studying me with concern, glanced out the window and said, "Here is Aubert so soon. We must be going." She took my arm in her strong hand and guided me along beside the wheel chair to the elevator.

Our leave taking was so abrupt, that I had not had the sense to thank Elsa for the check she had wanted me to have and had sent to grandfather, my own mother's aussteuer that in the orchid envelope had disappeared so mysteriously in the mail line at the American Express in Paris where Michael had pretended to befriend me.

Even as we were saying goodbye to Elsa and Hulda, three Volkswagons filled with Elsa's students were churning up the steep drive, easing around Elsa's tan and red van parked there.

CHAPTER 23

"You are very quiet, Daphne," Aunt Olivia said to me as Aubert expertly drove the big limousine down the steep and twisting road. "I know how emotional a meeting that was for you. I should have waited longer to bring you over."

"It was the pictures," I started involuntarily. I couldn't tell her about Michael. I could never tell anyone about Michael. I needed time to think it out. To find out why Michael would want to kill me.

"Yes, I know. Your mother was very lovely. It was tragic; star-crossed lovers. So many of them in the history of these two fine countries."

Aubert turned to us at a crossroad. "Do we accept the invitation to return to the Inn? They would enjoy it as I think you would."

"I would adore it, Aubert, and it would cheer you up, Daphne. How about it, my dear?"

I agreed instantly. I did not want to go back to the chateau until I had time to sort out my feelings and my thoughts. Aunt Olivia believed that it was seeing the pictures of mother that had upset me. Grandfather, who would want to hear all about the visit, would recognize my extreme distress.

"But I shall not be able to eat a bite, Aubert," Aunt Olivia told him about our meal that Hulda prepared and they began a discussion about German dishes.

My mind went back to the last time I saw Michael at the gangway to the ship. Michael had recognized Pierre. I knew that if Pierre had recognized Michael he would have told me right then before he learned of my encounter in Paris. Upon recognizing Pierre, Michael must have ducked into the cab and got away before Pierre would see him.

I began to tremble. Aunt Olivia stopped in the middle of a sentence about white sausages to place the lap robe over me. "It is turning cold, isn't it?" And went right on with her discussion with Aubert.

I knew now when Pierre went to the purser's office to find out if Michael Strange from Boston had made a reservation that he might have seen Frederich M. Weill's name on the registry. I wondered that he had not told me, if he had indeed seen it. And I recalled Michael's distress on the train when the passports were called for. Michael had a German passport, a different shade of green. And his friends had called him Fritz.

Michael. I could not make myself believe that that serious, too-old for his age young man would attempt to kill me. How could he have known that I would go to American Express? Perhaps he assumed when he received Elsa's letter that she most certainly must have sent to tell them about my father and the funeral, that Americans got their mail there. Probably she told him that she had already sent the check. He must have been standing there day after day in wait . . .

And the check must be large indeed for a cousin to want to kill a girl he had never seen to get it. I knew from his remarks about working his way through school and his desperate wish to operate on Elsa's back that a large sum would mean a great deal to him. Well, he could have it. I would never claim it now. Beyond anything else, I wanted to go home. Work would help me forget, and I had accumulated an awful lot to forget with my hurt over Michael, my hopeless love for Pierre, and my lost father.

I would never forget grandfather. I pondered asking him to go home with me for a visit so that he could see where his son had lived and worked. He would have to be stronger. We could work it out later.

For now, I had to come to terms with myself about Michael. I had loved him for his fineness. I couldn't connect his natural goodness with attempted murder. Once he had the check, why had he insisted upon going with me to the ship, getting a reservation for himself as far as Heidelberg? Why had he made such elaborate attempts to appear to be searching for the man who had stabbed me at American Express?

There was an answer. It did not come easy. And I could not find those cruel eyes in the face of the handsome Louis who was Elsa's twin. But for a while I let myself walk in Michael's shoes. Supposing Elsa was my sister, in need of an expensive operation she might not be able to afford. Then knowing of the keep affection between Louis and Elsa as twins, I could understand that Louis might have urged Elsa to keep quiet about the aussteuer their father had insisted upon saving in case mother ever returned to claim it. I could have met Elsa and gone away never knowing about it. Elsa, generous as she was, had been thrilled to act instantly upon hearing of my existence to send the money to me.

Why had she acted so swiftly? Had it been because she thought one or both of her brothers would object, and probably rightly? After all, mother had been gone since the beginning of the war, before their father married, before they were born. All through their struggles that money had been in the bank at Basel. I could imagine the times when they felt like drawing it out, believing mother long dead.

That Michael, a distraught and anxious young man, had been looking for his brother Louis, was my final conclusion. When he saw Pierre greet me on the gangway he knew Pierre would recognize him and be astounded to have him introduced as a Michael Strange of Boston. Also, he would know that Pierre would protect me. Which he had not if the man in the shop doorway had been Louis.

Trying to bring back the Louis of the pictures, I could not imagine those eyes I had seen in Paris in so sweet a face, but eyes can change expressions.

If my conjectures were true, then poor Jules, in a fit of anger or fear of having his affair with Theresa exposed, might have killed Antoine and Linette, probably had. With both mysteries finally explained, then I could go home . . .

We had reached the Inn and were soon surrounded by Aubert's charming friends. We were led into a large back parlor where a party was already in session. Couples were dancing to a small band. Beer was flowing freely. Laughter surrounded us. After meeting more people, Aubert led us out into a garden that had been decorated with strings of lights and lanterns. Tables and chairs were set up for dinner. The tantalizing fragrance of sauerkraut filled the air. I did not think then that I could eat a bite, but after dancing with most of the men present, an activity that lessened my tension, and a large amount of beer helped considerably so that by the time dinner was served, I joined the group.

During dinner, we were entertained by Black Forest dancers in native costume.

Although it was past midnight, Aimee was sitting up beside the window. "I didn't expect you to be so late. How did you find Elsa? She hasn't visited us for years. Such a pitiful girl."

"Not any more, Aimee. She has her classes and handwork to occupy her, and better still, she will soon have a husband."

"He'd better be a good man with compassion." She sat looking up at me. "You look tired, cherie. Get to bed. Your grandfather has planned another busy day for you."

My last thoughts were that tomorrow I would tell grandfather that I must get home to my shop. A way would come for me to explain that I couldn't accept mother's dowry.

The morning was beautiful. It should have been dark and foreboding to foretell the terror that would surround me before the day ended.

After my visit with grandfather during which I could not bring myself to tell him anything except about Elsa and our trip, I relieved Monsieur Rochelle in the clock room so that he could go to headquarters. Bertin kept me hard at work until teatime. At noon we shared liverwurst on dark bread while he instructed me in the art of self-defense with an empty slingshot.

It was at tea that Robert told me grandfather had asked him to give me a lesson. I had been uncomfortable with him since the morning Pierre and Nanette left.

"I'm sorry. I'm to visit the vineyards with Aunt Michele."

"Then I'll see you when you get back."

I had tried to conceal my disappointment that grandfather had chosen her to take me where Pierre had promised to be the guide.

Grandfather, as everyone else, was so pleased about Elsa's coming marriage that I could not find it in my heart to tell him I had decided to go home. Most certainly I would not stay on to be Elsa's bridesmaid when Michael would be there.

I excused myself to get my purse. I would want the grammar book that was in it for my French lesson.

Aunt Michele borrowed Father Andre's little pony and cart for our drive through the vineyards. They extended for miles and it wasn't possible for us to see all of it that lay beyond the buildings in countless rows of shimmering green.

By the time we had reached the buildings, I had learned that she did indeed know a great deal about growing grapes and winemaking. And she was intensely curious about Elsa.

Her eyes fairly popped when she leaned toward me to ask whom Elsa had chosen.

"I don't know. She didn't tell us his name. He's a student she met when she was working for her degree. Right now I think he is doing translating for a man in Paris."

"Then you don't know when the wedding will be held?"

"She told us that it would be Octoberfest."

When I looked over at her, tears were running down her cheeks. Taking the reins in one hand, she brushed at them with her sleeve.

"That was the time I had hoped that Pierre and Theresa would marry. Oh, Daphne, do be careful when you fall in love. I have been so busy with my own affairs that I failed to recognize that Theresa's dreams had turned elsewhere." I wondered that she didn't choke. If ever I had seen anyone take such close observation of the affairs of others, it was Aunt Michele.

"She does not intend to marry Pierre, has never given that any wish in spite of my urging that a marriage between them would assure the future of the chateau and the business. Her father, your Uncle Jean, took an active part. It was he who built up the business end. He was a good salesman and had a head for figures. Now I find that Theresa cares nothing for anything that Jean stood for. She, and you will hear this sooner or later so I may as well tell you now, is in love with Jules, who has no future whatever, and she vows to stand by him until he is cleared of the charges, which he will not be."

She had pulled in behind a line of grape wagons between the buildings, dropped the lines and was wiping at her eyes. All of the revulsion I had felt for her slipped away, and I put my arm around her shoulders.

"If they are in love, and it all works out, be happy for them. My father and mother had years of happiness in spite of having to leave their homelands to get it. Jules and Theresa might do the same." I did not tell her that grandfather was fond of Jules and certain of his innocence. Grandfather could do that in time when all was known. For now it was enough that I try to comfort her. "I saw Jules only once, and he seems to be an intelligent and sensitive young man who couldn't possibly murder those he loved."

She pulled her hands from her wet and agonized eyes. "Those were Jeannine Villiers' exact words. She told the police about Theresa and Jules and that Linette's mother had stalled the marriage which had been a family arrangement made when they were children. She recognized that Jules and Linette were more like brother and sister than sweethearts and she knew they would realize it in time. In spite of my shock and disbelief, I could not help but be proud of Theresa. She told the commissioner that it was true and that she had been with Jules at the time Linette was shot. The poor child."

"Then don't you see. There must be new evidence to prove his innocence."

"Claude said that. I thought he was just consoling an aging and foolish mother who wanted her child's life to be easier than mine. I don't know what possessed me to speak of this to you whose coming here I so deeply resented."

I knew. Out of my own grief I recognized that she couldn't turn to someone close. It had been to the stranger, Michael, that I had poured out my grief.

She tied the reins and patted the pony. "Thank you, Daphne. Come along and I'll show you the winery."

We entered into an old building of gigantic proportions, greatly redolent of heavy sugary wines, where stood the oak storage tanks that Pierre watched for cracks. From there we passed into the new grape-pressing plant that had to be built when the old one was destroyed in the war.

She explained to me how the grapes were dumped into the crushing hopper from a conveyer, skin, seeds and all and moved directly into fermenting tanks.

She took me into the office building closed for the weekend. We wandered up and down halls looking into offices and lounges. Everywhere we went everything was immaculately clean. Outside the office building, a parking place was surrounded with garden spots of tall trees shading benches and tables.

"Jean and your grandfather worked all of this out as the business increased. Shortly after the war ended Jean discovered that Claude was selling wines of ancient vintages for ridiculously low prices. He stepped in and from then on the chateau business was firm. Upon his death, Claude was lost." Her voice became wistful. "He sent for Caron who had struggled for so long with his own land and little funds that he came instantly. He has continued on in the way Jean did . . ."

We walked around the building and into the passageway where we had parked the ponycart.

"I wanted to show you the bottling plant and the cases of stored sparkling wines, but the key is not on the ring. I want to tell Claude that it is missing."

As we drove up to the chapel to return the borrowed pony and cart, Robert stood waiting with the sun flashing on his glasses, an air of extreme impatience about the way he stood . . .

CHAPTER 24

We chose one of the benches in the courtyard beyond the chapel. I sat with the grammar book closed on my lap while we went over phrases I had been studying in my spare time, mostly at night when I couldn't sleep.

Finally he said, "You're tired. Would you rather do this another day? Or perhaps you feel you know enough French?" There was some irony in his voice that annoyed me.

"Perhaps so. I shall have to go home soon. My shop is my livelihood and I must get back to it."

He tightened as if frozen, listening intently as if to reconstruct my words. "That's incredible." He waved a hand excitedly to encompass the chateau. "And leave all this wealth behind you? No girl in her right mind would do that. I suppose all of the accidents have made you feel that you must leave. I wonder about the sickle. Bertin is indeed a master with his slingshots . . ."

As he went on talking about it as if everyone knew about it when I was sure they did not or Aimee and grandfather would have been frightened and would certainly have asked me for details, I supposed that Bertin had been bragging about his prowess with the slingshot in spite of Monsieur Rochelle's warnings. Grandfather intrusted me into Robert's care. I looked upon him in a new light. Robert could be in Monsieur Rochelle's confidence. It was even possible that he was working with the police.

It had just come to me that this would be one person I could talk to about Michael. It would help me to discuss my fears and Robert had taken great interest in the other attacks on me, especially the one in Paris. And he was helping me bring it up by starting to question me about yesterday.

"You look so distressed, Daphne. It must have been hard on you visiting your mother's relatives."

"The boys weren't home, so there was only Elsa. She was most gracious."

"What did you do besides talk as all women do too much." His eyebrows rose as he gave an embarrassed laugh. "I didn't mean that you do. I have to pull information from you."

I told him about her home and the monkscloth curtains I hoped to make for my own home. He seemed so interested that I described them in detail.

"And did you find her well and happy?"

"Exceedingly so. She is to be married at Octoberfest."

"That is always good news and a right time for a wedding. I suppose she told you all about her fiance."

"No, nothing except that he was a student too when they met and that he works in Paris. She invited me to be her bridesmaid."

"And you will make a lovely one."

"I can't stay that long, besides her brothers will . . ." That was my opening to tell him of my troubled mind over Michael, but I lost the chance when a small voice behind us called out, "Here, sissy cat, come sissy cat," and I looked down to see the small girl we had encountered in the garden with her white kitten.

"Have you lost your kitten again?" I asked.

Robert studied me oddly. "You asked that so naturally that I'm sure you won't need further lessons." He got up. "Is Elsa planning to visit the chateau before you leave for home?"

By that time I was on my feet. The small white kitten raced toward the ruins to disappear over the edge of the moat with the child in fast pursuit. I reached her as she tumbled down the side. Picking her up, I placed her on the walk.

"Stay here until we catch your kitten. This is no place for little girls. You might fall again and be hurt." She started to whimper. By the time I chased down the moat for the kitten, she was crying loudly.

Robert was behind me when I ran down into the moat. The kitten leaped up on a wide wall just a foot above. Stepping up gingerly, I reached for it, but before I could catch it, it leaped to the steps above me and stared down as if daring me to follow. As long as I didn't look down at the river far below I would be fine. I climbed the steps and caught the kitten which slipped out of my hands and raced back toward the courtyard and the child. A woman had come to pick up both of them and wave to us.

"Now that you are up this far, come on to the top and see the view. It is one of the best on the river."

I hesitated as he climbed up to stand beside me. A car swept into the drive and I turned to see Pierre's red convertible pull up to the door of the clock-room corridor. Behind it, came a large tan and red Volkswagen such as I had seen in front of Elsa's home. Robert was urging me to come on up to the top when I saw Michael lift a wheelchair from the back of the Volkswagon.

I gasped and Robert turned to look. "Why, they're all here. Elsa, Michael, Louis and Pierre."

I started to run, wondering what could bring them at this time. "I'm going down. Something must have happened. Elsa distinctly told us she had classes every day this week."

"Go on then. I have an appointment in town." His voice was so deadly, so strangely gutteral, and so furious that I swung around to look at him and my purse hit his glasses sending them askew. I looked up into eyes that I knew I would never forget. I stared at him in terror that I couldn't conceal.

"You. Robert, you were the man in American Express."

With shaking hands, he adjusted his glasses and attempted to keep his voice normal. "I can't see without them, and you are being ridiculous."

It occurred to me that I *was* being ridiculous. What earthly reason would Robert have for wanting to kill me? Not long ago I had believed that he was working with the police.

I stood watching my cousins push Elsa's wheelchair inside. Had it just been Elsa and Pierre, I would have raced down to see them. But Michael and Louis . . . Had Michael, knowing that Louis had done those things to keep mother's money, made Louis come here?

Robert put out a hand when I started to hurry down the steps. He took a wild glance up at the top of the wall where moments before he had urged me to go, and then looked down into the moat. In the gathering twilight, the motion of his head brought back inexorably the man in American Express, and I started to let out one of my searing shrieks I had learned playing in the pueblo now so safe and so far away. In swift decision, Robert shoved me toward the moat with such force that I had no breath to call out. I landed face down in heavy brush as Robert dropped heavily beside me.

As he snatched me up and ran into the darkness of the old ruins, Nanette's words swept back reminding me that Robert looked more like an athlete than a teacher. He was frighteningly powerful as he tossed me to the stone floor of the room where father had had grandfather store his treasures. He began raging, and kicking me viciously. I tried to creep to the wall.

"I knew from the moment I heard the name Daphne Laurens that my plans were wrecked. Elsa and I were going to use that money to build our school. You've ruined everything. Elsa could have inherited your mother's share of the Laurens' estate if you had not come into the scene."

And could have if I had died, I realized. The bitterness of his voice tore through me. He was mad. I had had no experience with madness. Instinct to save myself told me to stay calm and to reason with him in the way women were now being taught to reason with an attacker.

"But I don't want the money. I have turned it down. I will never claim it because I have no right to it. It belongs to my uncle's children. Mother gave up any claim to it by leaving as she did. And I told you that I was going home."

He became more calm. He was thinking. I could almost hear him think in the deadly stillness of this stone tomb.

He let go a deep sigh. "Yes, out there in the courtyard

when you told me, I felt safe. But now with them coming . . ."

His rage intensified and he scuffled around hunting for me realizing now that I had slowly been creeping toward the last faint light of day, creeping through a nightmare that had descended upon me as one sleeping might try in vain to awaken.

A brutal blow with his foot caught my leg and I gasped. But my voice was cool and natural. "There is no need to tell anyone anything about this except that I fell. They are now used to me having accidents. I can go to my room and I will leave France tomorrow on the first flight. I know who you are, and I can see why you would resent my intrusion into your life the same way my relatives at the chateau resent me. I'm sorry I came, but I will leave. I promise."

He snatched me back from the opening and threw me so hard toward an unseen wall that my breath shot out in a cry.

"Keep quiet. And don't talk any more about leaving. The instant it is dark enough you will go over the top of the wall as I've been trying to make you do for days. I shall go into town. No one here knows my real name except Elsa and her brothers."

I didn't know where I hurt the worst, but I still had my purse dragging on my arm. It wasn't much of a weapon, but with the grammar book and my flashlight and all of the other things I carried with me, it was of considerable weight. If I could knock his glasses off, I might be able to get away. I knew and he might think of it any minute, that the only thing that could have brought the four of them rushing here to the chateau was that either Michael or Pierre or Michael and Pierre together had figured out that Elsa's fiance might also be interested in the money in the bank in Basel. It occurred to me that Elsa might have shown Pierre a picture of Robert, or whatever his name really was, and they came. They were here. And I would be fished up from the Rhine, murdered by a madman.

I was not going to be murdered if I could help it. I wanted to live past twenty. And I didn't want my death to bring further anguish to grandfather. Yes, and to Pierre who must have been away trying to solve this mystery. Even if he loved the fickle Nanette, he had evidently solved it, if in vain for me. It would not be wise for me to tell Robert that he would be tracked down in the end. And it certainly would not be wise to tell him that my dying would save Elsa a horrible life with a madman.

I had to keep my head. All I needed was to knock Robert out, not easy considering his strength. I had to stall him long enough for a search to begin which it surely would soon.

I tried to measure the distance to the opening which I could still make out dimly. I hesitated, wondering if I dared make a dash for it. I can run like the wind on the level, but not on that rough terrain and up those steep walls of the moat.

"Are you moving again? I told you to be quiet."

"I am being quiet. You've been kind to me since I came here, Robert. And I do understand how it is . . ."

"You couldn't possibly understand and you didn't fool me with your talk about throwing it all away to return to a dreary work life."

"Robert, there's enough money in that bank in Basel," a wild guess. "You and Elsa can have a good life if you have not yet committed a crime," I was not going to say murder. I doubted that he had a weapon on him or he would have used it by now. My own thoughts stopped me. I was to be found drowned, not stabbed or shot so that murder might be ruled out.

"Don't worry. I'm not going to commit murder. You are going to die a natural death by drowning."

He had read my mind. I supposed that madmen might consider drowning a natural death. I decided to try another tack, besides I was curious.

"How does it happen that you work here and no one knows your real name?"

"That was my plan from the moment I knew Elsa's aunt had married into such a wealthy family." There came a touch of pride in his voice. "Being a linguist, it was easy for me to go to Caron and offer my services in the business. I work well with people. I am accepted and trusted or I would not have been handling your grandfather's mail."

Grandfather's mail. He'd probably read my first letter. He might even had decided right then to eliminate all of us so that Elsa would inherit from my mother's claim.

While he talked on, I stopped listening and braced myself for my attack. Creeping slowly up the wall until I was on my feet, unsteadily, but on them, I moved toward his voice. In the dim outline of last light he was turned toward the opening and listening. Creeping toward him, I swung my purse with every ounce of strength that I had intending to swing past him and run out. But the soft tinkle of his breaking glasses was of little satisfaction when he shoved me the other direction.

I ran, feeling along the slimy wall with one hand that suddenly touched nothing. This opening could be the tunnel Aunt Olivia had shown me from the dumb waiter. It faced the right way. I raced down it, arms outstretched to touch the walls, my purse banging my hip, my breath coming in painful gasps from what felt like a couple of broken ribs.

In the blankness of terror and the panic of my rising waves of claustrophobia, I ran. Behind me I heard a grunt as if Robert had fallen, then a gutteral curse followed by the sound of his heavy footsteps running accompanied by a bumping sound as his heavy body struck the walls. My panic was so great that I felt I had to use the flashlight in my purse, but the second it would take to get it might be my last. Even in my terror, I felt pity for him, for the darkness that lay inexorably ahead of him. Perhaps his worry had driven him mad. He had seemed more normal when I arrived here than some of my relatives.

Seconds seemed hours. I had no way of knowing how far I had come. The distance would be no longer than a city block at home, as far as the ruins lay from the chateau, if this were the right tunnel and I didn't suddenly come to a dead end.

The footsteps behind me stopped as I came to a curve. I imagined I heard voices behind me. With him stopped, probably listening, I snatched the flashlight and turned the beam ahead.

Robert was running so close behind me that I could hear his labored breathing as my light fell upon crude ladder-like steps directly in front of me.

I clambered up, snatching each step above to keep my balance. Robert reached out for me. I kicked him. I didn't mean to kick him in the face. I hated doing it. I shouldn't have done it because simultaneously as I plunged through the dumb waiter a brilliant light, men's voices and the pounding of feet came down the passageway.

I shall never know who else was in the kitchen except Aimee who ran to me as the relief of oblivion swept over me.

CHAPTER 25

I opened my eyes as an icy towel touched my neck. Alphonse removed it and smiled down at me. Aimee was at my side, a kitchen jelly-glass of strong liquor in her hand. I didn't drink it, but stared at the dumb waiter as Pierre came through on his hands and knees, jumped up and ran to grab me in his arms, murmuring words that I will treasure forever.

Monsieur Rochelle and Commissioner Eitienne burst into the room at the moment Michael pushed a disheveled Robert through the dumb waiter. Robert got to his feet, straightened his back and spoke in a composed voice.

"I can't see any of you. Would someone please go to my room and get me another pair of glasses? They are in the handkerchief drawer on the right."

Thus it was in the kitchen that I met Louis. Michael brought him to me.

"Daphne, I am so sorry. You can never forgive me for not telling you who I was. When Elsa's letter came telling me about you and that you would be in Paris that week, I hung around the American Express office knowing that's where most American travelers get their mail. I didn't know the name of your hotel. I came,

234

hoping to be of service. When you were stabbed as I was coming to introduce myself, my first thought was Louis. he could have been in that crowd. He could have resented Elsa sending you the money. As for Steve, whom you know as Robert, neither Louis nor I had ever seen him."

I took his hands. "Michael, I understand. After I was stabbed, you were afraid to tell me. You wanted to see Louis first."

"I couldn't find him. Your description fit him except that I had never thought of his eyes as cruel."

Louis smiled down at me. "They aren't," I told them.

"Elsa gave Pierre the clue when she told him about Steve's eyes and the special glasses ground for him in Basel. She also told him she had sent the check instantly when Steve showed resentment that she didn't intend keeping it for her aussteuer."

Pierre pressed my shoulder. "I knew instantly. Robert had shown me the glasses when he came here from Caron. I'd never seen any like them. He's talented and likable. He had a good future here."

"I'm sorry for Elsa. I don't want her aussteuer."

"I should have called, but there was that chance that I was wrong. Robert, or Steve, I should say, usually answered the telephone. I knew if I called from Freiburg, he would know we were on to him. My hesitation almost got you killed."

Aimee interrupted. "Cherie, the doctor has come to look you over. And your grandfather is anxious to see you."

Two hours later Aimee and I joined Elsa in the library.

"Elsa, I am so deeply sorry."

She took my hand. "It is I who am sorry. I knew Steve's lust for money. He knew about the aussteuer in the bank. He thought we should have it. So many years had passed with no word of Aunt Elsa. I recognized Steve's acquisitiveness to my sorrow then, and to my great relief now, since money meant more to him than I did. Don't fret. I shan't shed a tear." She shuddered. "I'm lucky. I'm happy in my work. I'm just so thankful he didn't do more than break a few of your ribs."

She stopped when Aunt Olivia and grandfather came in. Since it was very late, we went in to dinner, this time in the main dreary dining room which would accommodate the extra guests. Pierre took his place beside me. It was over. Fear was gone. In spite of it, grandfather was grave and quiet. Caron hardly touched his food. The rest of us tried to keep up conversation. But there was a tension and we all felt it.

Aunt Olivia prevailed upon my cousins to spend the night and not drive back to Freiburg, but Elsa insisted upon being home for her pupils tomorrow.

Pierre and I went to the door with them. He promised Elsa to bring me to her home soon.

As they drove away, Pierre lifted my chin and looked into my face. "It isn't all over yet, Daphne. Claude wants us to join him in the library where he faces another ordeal. Monsieur Rochelle's interview with the gatekeeper the day of the sickle incident clarified that Robert and Caron went to the vineyard offices . . ." Nanette came out the door, her face flushed. As she rushed up to Pierre and clasped his hands, he said to me, "You'll hear it all in the library."

Nanette was saying goodbye. "Thank, old sport. As you know, if Caron isn't going to be wealthy, I don't want him. I'll be leaving in the morning."

"Sorry, Nanette. I caught the shortages at the vineyard office before Daphne came. I was in the midst of checking. I intended that Caron should meet Daphne. That would have given me the chance before calling in an expert."

Nanette smiled ruefully. "At least we fooled Michele. She has believed all along that I was your girl."

No, you didn't, I thought, remembering Aunt Michele trailing them that early morning. It had been Caron with Nanette.

That pleased me so much that I smiled. "With your beauty, Nanette, you could land a millionaire."

Stooping, she kissed me on each cheek. "If Pierre had been rich enough, he wouldn't be holding your hand now."

She flew up the staircase, her green gown trailing, and we both watched in admiration.

"It's a game with Nanette. She's been playing it all her life. As much as she wants money, she'll never marry. She would miss the adulation her modeling brings."

In the library Caron sat straight, his chiseled face ashen. As he addressed grandfather, he seemed unaware that Aunt Michele held his hand. "Claude, I considered them loans which I intend to repay. My estate was neglected in my absence. In truth, it was practically shot when I left. My mistakes were not to ask you for a loan, and worse, hiring Robert." He shook his head, and looked at me.

"Two fine people dead, and I am almost the cause of your death, Daphne."

Grandfather went to him. "I sent for you because I needed you, Caron. I didn't know you needed money, or I . . ."

"You don't really need me. Pierre can handle the business better than I. I'll leave as soon as I pack."

Aunt Michele clung to his arm. "I'm going with you, Caron. I can help you. With Theresa marrying Jules. Don't look so surprised. She's on her way into Strasbourg to bring him home. He was released when Robert admitted mistaking Antoine for Claude, and Linette because she wore Daphne's cape. He blamed everything except blackmailing Caron on his poor eyesight, especially missing Daphne with that sickle."

Aunt Celeste buried her face in her hands. "It's too horrible. I can't bear it. Claude, I should like to travel."

"And you shall, Celeste. I've been selfish because of my need for family. You've earned a long vacation."

She reached out and took my hand. "Daphne, will you take over for me? Since Pierre wants to marry you . . ."

"Mother."

Aunt Celeste merely smiled at him as her eyes wistfully followed Caron and Michele out of the room.

In my daze I realized that Aunt Michele would be a great help to Caron in building up his own estate where Aunt Olivia and I had seen Pierre's car. And, as I had believed ever since I got here, they deserved each other.

Alphonse, who had been standing inside the dining room door listening, strode in with an ancient bottle of brandy.

'It occurs to me that someone might wish to offer a toast." He stood smiling toward the doorway Caron had passed through.

Grandfather pulled the bell cord. Aunt Olivia came in with Aimee.

"We listened at the door, Claude," she blurted in her wonderful open way. Then she grabbed Pierre and me

238

and kissed us. "I don't have to wait to hear Daphne's answer. I've been watching all along and I knew."

Words were beyond me, but I knew too. As we were congratulated and toasted, I listened in wonder as she and grandfather planned our wedding reception in the new white and gold ballroom.

PREFERRED CUSTOMERS!

Leisure Books and Love Spell
proudly present
a brand-new catalogue and a
TOLL-FREE NUMBER

STARTING JUNE 1, 1995
CALL 1-800-481-9191
between 2:00 and 10:00 p.m.
(Eastern Time)
Monday Through Friday

GET A FREE CATALOGUE
AND ORDER BOOKS USING
VISA AND MASTERCARD

LEISURE BOOKS   **LOVE SPELL**